BADGE OF INFAMY

MORE WILDSIDE CLASSICS

BADGE OF INFAMY

LESTER DEL REY

WILDSIDE PRESS

BADGE OF INFAMY

BADGE OF INFAMY

I

PARIAH

The air of the city's cheapest flophouse was thick with the smells of harsh antiseptic and unwashed bodies. The early Christmas snowstorm had driven in every bum who could steal or beg the price of admission, and the long rows of cots were filled with fully clothed figures. Those who could afford the extra dime were huddled under thin, grimy blankets.

The pariah who had been Dr. Daniel Feldman enjoyed no such luxury. He tossed fitfully on a bare cot, bringing his face into the dim light. It had been a handsome face, but now the black stubble of beard lay over gaunt features and sunken cheeks. He looked ten years older than his scant thirty-two, and there were the beginnings of a snarl at the corners of his mouth. Clothes that had once been expensive were wrinkled and covered with grime that no amount of cleaning could remove. His tall, thin body was awkwardly curled up in a vain effort to conserve heat and one of his hands instinctively clutched at his tiny bag of possessions.

He stirred again, and suddenly jerked upright with a protest already forming on his lips. The ugly surroundings registered on his eyes, and he stared suspiciously at the other cots. But there was no sign that anyone had been trying to rob him of his bindle or the precious bag of cheap tobacco.

He started to relax back onto the couch when a sound caught his attention, even over the snoring of the others. It was a low wail, the sound of a man who can no longer control himself.

Feldman swung to the cot on his left as the moan hacked off. The man there was well fed and clean-shaven, but his face was gray with sickness. He was writhing and clutching his stomach, arching his back against the misery inside him.

"Space-stomach?" Feldman diagnosed.

He had no need of the weak answering nod. He'd treated such cases several times in the past. The disease was usually caused by the absence of gravity out in space, but it could be brought on later from abuse of the weakened internal organs, such as the intake of too much bad liquor. The man must have been frequenting the wrong space-front bars.

Now he was obviously dying. Violent peristaltic contractions seemed to be tearing the intestines out of him, and the paroxysms were coming faster. His eyes darted to Feldman's tobacco sack and there was animal appeal in them.

Feldman hesitated, then reluctantly rolled a smoke. He held the cigarette while the spaceman took a long, gasping drag on it. He smoked the remainder himself, letting the harsh tobacco burn against his lungs and sicken his empty stomach. Then he shrugged and threaded his way through the narrow aisles toward the attendant.

"Better get a doctor," he said bitterly, when the young punk looked up at him. "You've got a man dying of space-stomach on 214."

The sneer on the kid's face deepened. "Yeah? We don't pay for doctors every time some wino wants to throw up. Forget it and get back where you belong, bo."

"You'll have a corpse on your hands in an hour," Feldman insisted. "I know space-stomach, damn it."

The kid turned back to his lottery sheet. "Go treat yourself if you wanta play doctor. Go on, scram—before I toss you out in the snow!"

One of Feldman's white-knuckled hands reached for the attendant. Then he caught himself. He started to turn back, hesitated, and finally faced the kid again. "I'm not fooling. And I *was* a doctor," he stated. "My name is Daniel Feldman."

The attendant nodded absently, until the words finally penetrated. He looked up, studied Feldman with surprised curiosity and growing contempt, and reached for the phone. "Gimme Medical Directory," he muttered.

Feldman felt the kid's eyes on his back as he stumbled through the aisles to his cot again. He slumped down, rolling another cigarette in hands that shook. The sick man was approaching delirium now, and the moans were mixed with weak whining sounds of fear. Other men had wakened and were watching, but nobody made a move to help.

The retching and writhing of the sick man had begun to weaken, but it was still not too late to save him. Hot water and skillful massage could interrupt the paroxysms. In fifteen minutes, Feldman could have stopped the attack completely.

He found his feet on the floor and his hands already reaching out. Savagely he pulled himself back. Sure, he could save the man—and wind up in the gas chamber! There'd be no mercy for his second offense against Lobby laws. If the spaceman lived, Feldman might get off with a flogging—that was standard punishment for a pariah who stepped out of line. But with his luck, there would be a heart arrest and another juicy story for the papers.

Idealism! The Medical Lobby made a lot out of the word. But it wasn't for him. A pariah had no business thinking of others.

As Feldman sat there staring, the spaceman grew quieter. Sometimes, even at this stage, massage could help. It was harder without liberal supplies of hot water, but the massage was the really important treatment. It was the trembling of Feldman's hands that stopped him. He no longer had the strength or the certainty to make the massage effective.

He was glaring at his hands in self-disgust when the legal doctor arrived. The man was old and tired. Probably he had been another idealist who had wound up defeated, content to leave things up to the established procedures of the Medical Lobby. He looked it as he bent over the dying man.

The doctor turned back at last to the attendant. "Too late. The best I can do is ease his pain. The call should have been made half an hour earlier."

He had obviously never handled space-stomach before. He administered a hypo that probably held narconal. Feldman watched, his guts tightening sympathetically for the shock that would be to the sick man. But at least it would shorten his sufferings. The final seizure lasted only a minute or so.

"Hopeless," the doctor said. His eyes were clouded for a moment, and then he shrugged. "Well, I'll make out a death certificate. Anyone here know his name?"

His eyes swung about the cots until they came to rest on Feldman. He frowned, and a twisted smile curved his lips.

"Feldman, isn't it? You still look something like your pictures. Do you know the deceased?"

Feldman shook his head bitterly. "No. I don't know his name. I don't even know why he wasn't cyanotic at the end, *if* it was space-stomach. Do you, doctor?"

The old man threw a startled glance at the corpse. Then he shrugged and nodded to the attendant. "Well, go through his things. If he still has a space ticket, I can get his name from that."

The kid began pawing through the bag that had fallen from the cot. He dragged out a pair of shoes, half a bottle of cheap rum, a wallet and a bronze space ticket. He wasn't quick enough with the wallet, and the doctor took it from him.

"Medical Lobby authorization. If he has any money, it covers my fee and the rest goes to his own Lobby." There were several bills, all of large denominations. He turned the ticket over and began filling in the death certificate. "Arthur Billings. Space Lobby. Crewman. Cause of death, idiopathic gastroenteritis *and* delirium tremens."

There had been no evidence of delirium tremens, but apparently the doctor felt he had scored a point. He tossed the space ticket toward the shoes, closed his bag, and prepared to leave.

"Hey, doc!" The attendant's voice was indignant. "Hey, what about my reporting fee?"

The doctor stopped. He glanced at the kid, then toward Feldman, his face a mixture of speculation and dislike. He took a dollar bill from the wallet. "That's right," he admitted. "The fee for reporting a solvent case. Medical Lobby rules apply—even to a man who breaks them."

The kid's hand was out, but the doctor dropped the dollar onto Feldman's cot. "There's your fee, pariah." He left, forcing the protesting attendant to precede him.

Feldman reached for the bill. It was blood money for letting a man die—but it meant cigarettes and food—or shelter for another night, if he could get a mission meal. He no longer could afford pride. Grimly, he pocketed the bill, staring at the face of the dead man. It looked back sightlessly, now showing a faint speckling of tiny dots. They caught Feldman's eyes, and he bent closer. There should be no black dots on the skin of a man who died of space-stomach. And there should have been cyanosis. . . .

He swore and bent down to find the wrecks of his shoes. He couldn't worry about anything now but getting away from here before the attendant made trouble. His eyes rested on the shoes of the dead man—sturdy boots that would last for another year. They could do the corpse no good; someone else would steal them if he didn't. But he hesitated, cursing himself.

The right boot fitted better than he could have expected, but something got in the way as he tried to put the left one on. His fingers found the bronze ticket. He turned it over, considering it. He wasn't ready to fraud his identity for what he'd heard of life on the spaceships, yet. But he shoved it into his pocket and finished lacing the boots.

Outside, the snow was still falling, but it had turned to slush, and the sidewalk was soggy underfoot. There was going to be no work shoveling snow, he realized. This would melt before the day was over. Feldman hunched the suitcoat up, shivering as the cold bit into him. The boots felt good, though; if he'd had socks, they would have been completely comfortable.

He passed a cheap restaurant, and the smell of the synthetics set his stomach churning. It had been two days since his last real meal, and the dollar burned in his pocket. But he had to wait. There was a fair chance this early that he could scavenge something edible.

He shuffled on. After a while, the cold bothered him less, and he passed through the hunger spell. He rolled another smoke and sucked at it, hardly thinking. It was better that way.

It was much later when the big caduceus set into the sidewalk snapped him back to awareness of where he'd traveled. His undirected feet had led him much too far uptown, following old habits. This was the Medical Lobby building, where he'd spent more than enough time, including three weeks in custody before they stripped him of all rank and status.

His eyes wandered to the ornate entrance where he'd first emerged as a pariah. He'd meant to walk down those steps as if he were still a man. But each step had drained his resolution, until he'd finally covered his face and slunk off, knowing himself for what the world had branded him.

He stood there now, staring at the smug young medical politicians and the tired old general practitioners filing in and out. One of the latter halted, fumbled in his pocket and drew out a quarter.

"Merry Christmas!" he said dully.

Feldman fingered the coin. Then he saw a gray Medical policeman watching him, and he knew it was time to move on. Sooner or later, someone would recognize him here.

He clutched the quarter and turned to look for a coffee shop that sold the synthetics to which his metabolism had been switched. No shop would serve him here, but he could buy coffee and a piece of cake to take out.

A flurry of motion registered from the corner of his eye, and he glanced back.

"Taxi! Taxi!"

The girl rushing down the steps had a clear soprano voice, cultured and commanding. The gray Medical uniform seemed molded to her shapely figure and her red hair glistened in the lights of the street. Her snub nose and determined mouth weren't the current fashion, but nobody stopped to think of fashions when they saw her. She didn't have to be the daughter of the president of Medical Lobby to rule.

It was Chris—Chris Feldman once, and now Chris Ryan again.

Feldman swung toward a cab. For a moment, his attitude was automatic and assured, and the cab stopped before the driver noticed his clothes. He picked up the bag Chris dropped and swung it onto the front seat. She was fumbling in her change purse as he turned back to shut the door.

"Thank you, my good man," she said. She could be gracious, even to a pariah, when his homage suited her. She dropped two quarters into his hand, raising her eyes.

Recognition flowed into them, followed by icy shock. She yanked the cab door shut and shouted something to the driver. The cab took off with a rush that left Feldman in a backwash of slush and mud.

He glanced down at the coins in his hand. It was his lucky day, he thought bitterly.

He moved across the street and away, not bothering about the squeal of brakes and the honking horns. He looked back only once, toward the glowing sign that topped the building. *Your health is our business!* Then the great symbol of the health business faded behind him, and he stumbled on, sucking incessantly at the cigarettes he rolled. One hand clutched the bronze badge belonging to the dead man and his stolen boots drove onward through the melting snow.

It was Christmas in the year 2100 on the protectorate of Earth.

II

LOBBY

Feldman had set his legs the problem of heading for the great spaceport and escape from Earth, and he let them take him without further guidance. His mind was wrapped up in a whirl of the past—his past and that of the whole planet. Both pasts had in common the growth and sudden ruin of idealism.

Idealism! Throughout history, some men had sought the ideal, and most had called it freedom. Only fools expected absolute freedom, but wise men dreamed up many systems of relative freedom, including democracy. They had tried that in America, as the last fling of the dream. It had been a good attempt, too.

The men who drew the Constitution had been pretty practical dreamers. They came to their task after a bitter war and a worse period of wild chaos, and they had learned where idealism stopped and idiocy began. They set up a republic with all the elements of democracy that they considered safe. It had worked well enough to make America the number one power of the world. But the men who followed the framers of the new plan were a different sort, without the knowledge of practical limits.

The privileges their ancestors had earned in blood and care became automatic rights. Practical men tried to explain that there were no such rights—that each generation had to pay for its rights with responsibility. That kind of talk didn't get far. People wanted to hear about rights, not about duties.

They took the phrase that all men were created equal and left out the implied kicker that equality was in the sight of God and before the law. They wanted an equality with the greatest men without giving up their drive toward mediocrity, and they meant to have it. In a way, they got it.

They got the vote extended to everyone. The man on subsidy or public dole could vote to demand more. The man who read of nothing beyond sex crimes could vote on the great political issues of the world. No ability was needed for his vote. In fact, he was assured that voting alone was enough to make him a fine and noble citizen. He loved that, if he bothered to vote at all that year. He became a great man by listing his unthought, hungry desire for someone to take care of him without responsibility. So he went out and voted for the man who promised him most, or who looked most like what his limited dreams felt to be a father image or son image or hero image. He never bothered later to see how the men he'd elected had handled the jobs he had given them.

Someone had to look, of course, and someone did. Organized special interests stepped in where the mob had failed. Lobbies grew up. There had always been pressure groups, but now they developed into a third arm of the government.

The old Farm Lobby was unbeatable. The big farmers shaped the laws they wanted. They convinced the little farmers it was for the good of all, and they made the story stick well enough to swing the farm vote. They made the laws when it came to food and crops.

The last of the great lobbies was Space, probably. It was an accident that grew up so fast it never even knew it wasn't a real part of the government. It developed during a period of chaos when another country called Russia got the first hunk of metal above the atmosphere and when the representatives who had been picked for everything but their grasp of science and government went into panic over a myth of national prestige.

The space effort was turned over to the aircraft industry, which had never been able to manage itself successfully except under the stimulus of war or a threat of war. The failing airplane industry became the space combine overnight, and nobody kept track of how big it was, except a few sharp operators.

They worked out a system of subcontracts that spread the profits so wide that hardly a company of any size in the country wasn't getting a share. Thus a lot of patriotic, noble voters got their pay from companies in the lobby block and could be panicked by the lobby at the first mention of recession.

So Space Lobby took over completely in its own field. It developed enough pressure to get whatever appropriations it wanted, even over Presidential veto. It created the only space experts, which meant that the men placed in government agencies to regulate it came from its own ranks.

The other lobbies learned a lot from Space.

There had been a medical lobby long before, but it had been a conservative group, mostly concerned with protecting medical autonomy and ethics. It also tried to prevent government control of treatment and payment, feeling that it couldn't trust the people to know where to stop. But its history was a long series of retreats.

It fought what it called socialized medicine. But the people wanted their troubles handled free—which meant by government spending, since that could be added to the national debt, and thus didn't seem to cost anything. It lost, and eventually the government paid most medical costs, with doctors working on a fixed fee. Then quantity of treatment paid, rather than quality. Competence no longer mattered so much. The Lobby lost, but didn't know it—because the lowered standards of competence in the profession lowered the caliber of men running the political aspects of that profession as exemplified by the Lobby.

It took a worldwide plague to turn the tide. The plague began in old China; anything could start there, with more than a billion people huddled in one area and a few madmen planning to conquer the world. It might have been a laboratory mutation, but nobody could ever prove it.

It wiped out two billion people, depopulated Africa and most of Asia, and wrecked Europe, leaving only America comparatively safe to take over. An obscure scientist in one of the laboratories run by the Medical Lobby found a cure before the first waves of the epidemic hit America. Rutherford Ryan, then head of the Lobby, made sure that Medical Lobby got all the credit.

By the time the world recovered, America ran it and the Medical Lobby was untouchable. Ryan made a deal with Space Lobby, and the two effectively ran the world. None of the smaller lobbies could buck them, and neither could the government.

There was still a president and a congress, as there had been a Senate under the Roman Caesars. But the two Lobbies ran themselves as they chose. The real government had become a kind of oligarchy, as it always did after too much false democracy ruined the ideals of real and practical self-rule. A man belonged to his Lobby, just as a serf had belonged to his feudal landlord.

It was a safe world now. Maybe progress had been halted at about the level of 1980, but so long as the citizens didn't break the rules of their lobbies, they had very little to worry about. For that, for security and the right not to think, most people were willing to leave well enough alone.

Some rules seemed harsh, of course, such as the law that all operations had to be performed in Lobby hospitals. But that could be justified; it was the only safe kind of surgery and the only way to make sure there was no unsupervised experimentation, such as that which supposedly caused the plague. The rule was now an absolute ethic of medicine. It also made for better fees.

Feldman's father had stuck by the rule but had questioned it. Feldman learned not to question in medical school. He scored second in Medical Ethics only to Christina Ryan.

He had never figured why she singled him out for her attentions, but he gloried in both those attentions and the results. He became automatically a rising young man, the favorite of the daughter of the Lobby president. He went through internship without a sign of trouble. Chris humored him in his desire to spend three years of practice in a poor section loaded with disease, and her father approved; such selfless dedication was the perfect image projection for a future son-in-law. In return, he agreed to follow that period by becoming an administrator. A doctor's doctor, as they put it.

They were married in April and his office was ready in May, complete with a staff of eighty. The publicity releases had gone out, and the Public Relations Lobby that handled news and education was paid to begin the greatest buildup any young genius ever had.

They celebrated that, with a little party of some four hundred people and reporters at Ryan's lodge in Canada. It was to be a gala weekend.

It was then that Baxter shot himself.

Baxter had been Feldman's closest friend in the Lobby. He'd come along to handle press relations and had gotten romantic about the countryside, never having been out of a city before. He hired a guide and went hunting, eighty miles beyond the last outpost of civilization. Somehow, he got his hand on a gun, though only guides were supposed to touch them, managed to overcome its safety devices, and then pulled the trigger with the gun pointed the wrong way.

Chris, Feldman and Harnett from Public Relations had accompanied him on the trip. They were sitting in a nearby car while Feldman enjoyed the scenery, Chris made further plans, and Harnett gathered material. There was also a photographer and writer, but they hadn't been introduced by name.

Feldman reached Baxter first. The man was moaning and scared, and he was bleeding profusely. Only a miracle had saved him from instant death. The bullet had struck a rib, been deflected and robbed of some of its energy, and had barely reached the heart. But it had pierced the pericardium, as best Feldman could guess, and it could be fatal at any moment.

He'd reached for a probe without thinking. Chris knocked his hand aside.

She was right, of course. He couldn't operate outside a hospital. But they had no phone in the lodge where the guide lived and no way to summon an ambulance. They'd have to drive Baxter back in the car, which would almost certainly result in his death.

When Feldman seemed uncertain, Harnett had given his warning in a low but vehement voice. "You touch him, Dan, and I'll spread it in every one of our media. I'll have to. It's the only way to retain public confidence. There'd be a leak, with all the guides and others here, and we can't afford that. I like you—you have color. But touch that wound and I'll crucify you."

Chris added her own threats. She'd spent years making him the outlet for all her ambitions, denied because women were still only second-rate members of Medical Lobby. She couldn't let it go now. And she was probably genuinely shocked.

Baxter groaned again and started to bleed more profusely.

There wasn't much equipment. Feldman operated with a pocketknife sterilized in a bottle of expensive Scotch and only anodyne tablets in place of anesthesia. He got the bullet out and sewed up the wound with a bit of surgical thread he'd been using to tie up a torn good-luck emblem. The photographer and writer recorded the whole thing. Chris swore harshly and beat her fists against the bole of a tree. But Baxter lived. He recovered completely, and was shocked at the heinous thing that had been done to him.

They crucified Feldman.

III

SPACEMAN

Most crewmen lived rough, ugly lives—and usually, short ones. Passengers and officers on the big tubs were given the equivalent of gravity in spinning compartments, but the crews rode "free". The lucky crewmen lived through their accidents, got space-stomach now and then, and recovered. Nobody cared about the others.

Feldman's ticket was work-stamped for the *Navaho*, and nobody questioned his identity. He suffered through the agony of acceleration on the shuttle up to the orbital station, then was sick as acceleration stopped. But he was able to control himself enough to follow other crewmen down a hall of the station toward the *Navaho*. The big ships never touched a planet, always docking at the stations.

A checker met the crew and reached for their badges. He barely glanced at them, punched a mark for each on his checkoff sheet, and handed them back. "Deckmen forward, tubemen to the rear," he ordered. "*Navaho* blasts in fifteen minutes. Hey, you! You're tubes."

Feldman grunted. He should have expected it. Tubemen had the lowest lot of all the crew. Between the killing work, the heat of the tubes, and occasional doses of radiation, their lives weren't worth the metal value of their tickets.

He began pulling himself clumsily along a shaft, dodging freight the loaders were tossing from hand to hand. A bag hit his head, drawing blood, and another caught him in the groin.

"Watch it, bo," a loader yelled at him. "You dent that bag and they'll brig you. Cantcha see it's got a special courtesy stripe?"

It had a brilliant green stripe, he saw. It also had a name, printed in block letters that shouted their identity before he could read the words. *Dr. Christina Ryan, Southport, Mars.*

And he'd had to choose this time to leave Earth!

Suddenly he was glad he was assigned to the tubes. It was the one place on the ship where he'd be least likely to run into her. As a doctor and a courtesy passenger, she'd have complete run of the ship, but she'd hardly bother with the dangerous and unpleasant tube section.

He dragged his way back, beginning to sweat with the effort. The *Navaho* was an old ship. A lot of the handholds were missing, and he had to throw himself along by erratic leaps. He was gaining proficiency, but not enough to handle himself if the ship blasted off. Time was growing short when he reached the aft bunkroom where the other tubemen were waiting.

"Ben," one husky introduced himself. "Tube chief. Know how to work this?"

Feldman could see that they were assembling a small still. He'd heard of the phenomenal quantities of beer spacemen drank, and now he realized what really happened to it. Hard liquor was supposed to be forbidden, but they made their own. "I can work it," he decided. "I'm—uh—Dan."

"Okay, Dan." Ben glanced at the clock. "Hit the sacks, boys."

By the time Feldman could settle into the sacklike hammock, the *Navaho* began to shake faintly, and weight piled up. It was mild compared to that on the shuttle, since the big ships couldn't take high acceleration. Space had been conquered for more than a century, but the ships were still flimsy tubs that took months to reach Mars, using immense amounts of fuel. Only the valuable plant hormones from Mars made commerce possible at the ridiculously high freight rate.

Three hours later he began to find out why spacemen didn't seem to fear dying or turning pariah. The tube quarters had grown insufferably hot during the long blast, but the main tube-room was blistering as Ben led the men into it. The chief handed out spacesuits and motioned for Dan.

"Greenhorn, aincha? Okay, I'll take you with me. We go out in the tubes and pull the lining. I pry up the stuff, you carry it back here and stack it."

They sealed off the tube-room, pumped out the air, and went into the steaming, mildly radioactive tubes, just big enough for a man on hands and knees. Beyond the tube mouth was empty space, waiting for the man who slipped. Ben began ripping out the eroded blocks with a special tool. Feldman carried them back and stacked them along with others. A plasma furnace melted them down into new blocks. The work grew progressively worse as the distance to the tube-room increased. The tube mouth yawned closer and closer. There were no handholds there—only the friction of a man's body in the tube.

Life settled into a dull routine of labor, sleep, and the brief relief of the crude white mule from the still.

They were six weeks out and almost finished with the tube cleaning when Number Two tube blew. Bits of the remaining radioactive fuel must have collected slowly until they reached blow-point. Feldman in Number One would have gone sailing out into space, but Ben reacted at once. As the ship leaped slightly, Feldman brought up sharply against the chief's braced body. For a second their fate hung in the balance. Then it was over, and Ben shoved him back, grinning faintly.

He jerked his thumb and touched helmets briefly. "There they go, Dan."

The two men who had been working in Number Two were charred lumps, drifting out into space.

No further comment was made on it, except that they'd have to work harder from now on, since they were short-handed.

That rest period Feldman came down with a mild attack of space-stomach—which meant no more drinking for him—and was off work for a day. Then the pace picked up. The tubes were cleared and they began laying the new lining for the landing blasts. There was no time for thought after that. Mars' orbital station lay close when the work was finished.

Ben slapped Feldman on the back. "Ya ain't bad for a greenie, Dan. We all get six-day passes on Mars. Hit the sack now so you won't waste time sleeping then. We'll hear it when the ship berths."

Feldman didn't hear it, but the others did. He felt Ben shaking his shoulder, trying to drag him out of the sack. "Grab your junk, Dan."

Ben picked up Feldman's nearly empty bag and tossed it toward him, before his eyes were fully open. He grabbed for it and missed. He grabbed again, with Ben's laughter in his ears. The bag hit the wall and fell open, spilling its contents.

Feldman began gathering it up, but the chief was no longer laughing. A big hand grabbed up the space ticket suddenly, and there was no friendliness now on Ben's face.

"Art Billing's card!" Ben told the other tubemen. "Five trips I made with Art. He was saving his money, going to buy a farm on Mars. Five trips and one more to go before he had enough. Now you show up with his ticket!"

The tubemen moved forward toward Feldman. There was no indecision. To them, apparently, trial had been held and sentence passed.

"Wait a minute," Feldman began. "Billings died of—"

A fist snaked past his raised hand and connected with his jaw. He bounced off a wall. A wrench sailed toward him, glanced off his arm, and ripped at his muscles. Another heavy fist struck.

Abruptly, Ben's voice cut through their yells. "Hold it!" He shoved through the group, tossing men backwards. "Stow it! We can take care of him later. Right now, this is captain's business. You fools want to lose your leave?" He indicated two of the others. "You two bring him along—and keep him quiet!"

The two grabbed Feldman's arms and dragged him along as the chief began pulling his way forward through the tubes up towards the control section of the ship. Feldman took a quick glance at their faces and made no effort to resist; they obviously would have enjoyed any chance to subdue him.

They were stopped twice by minor officers, then sent on. They finally found the captain near the exit lock, apparently assisting the passengers to leave. Most of them went on into the shuttle, but Chris Ryan remained behind as the captain listened to Ben's report and inspected the false ticket.

Finally the captain turned to Feldman. "You. What's your name?"

Chris' eyes were squarely on Feldman, cold and furious. "He *was* Doctor Daniel Feldman, Captain Marker," she stated.

Feldman stood paralyzed. He'd been unwilling to face

Chris. He wanted to avoid all the past. But the idea that she would denounce him had never entered his head. There was no Medical rule involved. She knew that as a pariah he was forbidden to board a passenger ship, of course. But she'd been his wife once!

Marker bowed slightly to her. "Thank you, Dr. Ryan. I should take this criminal back to Earth in chains, I suppose. But he's hardly worth the freightage. You men. Want to take him down to Mars and ground him there?"

Ben grinned and touched his forelock. "Thank you, sir. We'd enjoy that."

"Good. His pay reverts to the ship's fund. That's all, men."

Feldman started to protest, but a fist lashed savagely against his mouth.

He made no other protests as they dragged him into the crew shuttle that took off for Southport. He avoided their eyes and sat hunched over. It was Ben who finally broke the silence.

"What happened to Art's money? He had a pile on him."

"Go to hell!"

"Give, I said!" Ben twisted his arm back toward his shoulder, applying increasing pressure.

"A doctor took it for his fee when Billings died of space-stomach. Damn you, I couldn't help him!"

Ben looked at the others. "Med Lobby fee, eh? All the market will take. Umm. It could be, maybe." He shrugged. "Okay, reasonable doubt. We won't kill you, bo. Not quite, we won't."

The shuttle landed and Ben handed out the little helmets and aspirators that made life possible in Mars' thin air. Outside, the tubemen took turns holding Feldman and beating him while the passengers disembarked from their shuttle. As he slumped into unconsciousness, he had a

picture of Chris Ryan's frozen face as she moved steadily toward the port station.

IV

MARTIAN

It was night when Feldman came to, and the temperature was dropping rapidly. He struggled to sit up through a fog of pain. Somewhere in his bag, he should have an anodyne tablet that would kill any ache. He finally found the pill and swallowed it, fumbling with the aspirator lip opening.

The aspirator meant life to him now, he suddenly realized. He twisted to stare at the tiny charge-indicator for the battery. It showed half-charge. Then he saw that someone had attached another battery beside it. He puzzled briefly over it, but his immediate concern was for shelter.

Apparently he was still where he had been knocked out. There was a light coming from the little station, and he headed toward that, fumbling for the few quarters that represented his entire fortune.

Maybe it would have been better if the tubemen had killed him. Batteries were an absolute necessity here, food and shelter would be expensive, and he had no skills to earn his way. At most, he had only a day or so left. But meantime, he had to find warmth before the cold killed him.

The tiny restaurant in the station was still open, and the air was warm inside. He pulled off the aspirator, shutting off the battery.

The counterman didn't even glance up as he entered. Feldman gazed at the printed menu and flinched.

"Soup," he ordered. It was the cheapest item he could find.

The counterman stared at him, obviously spotting his Earth origin. "You adjusted to synthetics?"

Feldman nodded. Earth operated on a mixed diet, with synthetics for all who couldn't afford the natural foods there. But Mars was all synthetic. Many of the chemicals in food could exist in either of two forms, or isomers; they were chemically alike, but differently crystallized. Sometimes either form was digestible, but frequently the body could use only the isomer to which it was adjusted.

Martian plants produced different isomers from those on Earth. Since the synthetic foods turned out to be Mars-normal, that was probably the more natural form. Research designed to let the early colonists live off native food here had turned up an enzyme that enabled the body to handle either isomer. In a few weeks of eating Martian or synthetic food, the body adapted; without more enzyme, it lost its power to handle Earth-normal food.

The cheapness of synthetics and the discovery that many diseases common to Earth would not attack Mars-normal bodies led to the wide use of synthetics on Earth. No pariah could have been expected to afford Earth-normal.

Feldman finished the soup, and found a cigarette that was smokable. "Any objections if I sit in the waiting room?"

He'd expected a rejection, but the counterman only shrugged. The waiting room was almost dark and the air was chilly, but there was normal pressure. He found a bench and slumped onto it, lighting his cigarette. He'd miss the smokes—but probably not for long. He finished the cigarette reluctantly and sat huddled on the bench, waiting for morning.

The airlock opened later, and feet sounded on the boards of the waiting-room floor, but he didn't look up until a thin beam of light hit him. Then he sighed and nodded. The shoes, made of some odd fiber, didn't look like those of a cop, but this was Mars. He could see only a hulking shadow behind the light.

"You the man who was a medical doctor?" The voice was dry and old.

"Yeah," Feldman answered. "Once."

"Good. Thought that space crewman was just lying drunk at first. Come along, Doc."

"Why?" It didn't matter, but if they wanted him to move on, they'd have to push a little harder.

The light swung up to show the other. He was the shade of old leather with a bleached patch of sandy hair and the gray eyes Feldman had ever seen. It was a face that could have belonged to a country storekeeper in New England, with the same hint of dry humor. The man was dressed in padded levis and a leather jacket of unguessable age. His aspirator seemed worn and patched, and one big hand fumbled with it.

"Because we're friends, Doc," the voice drawled at him. "Because you might as well come with us as sit here. Maybe we have a job for you."

Feldman shrugged and stood up. If the man was a Lobby policeman, he was different from the usual kind. Nothing could be worse than the present prospects.

They went out through the doors of the waiting room toward a rattletrap vehicle. It looked something like a cross between a schoolboy's jalopy and a scaled-down army tank of former times. The treads were caterpillar style, and the stubby body was completely enclosed. A tiny airlock stuck out from the rear.

Two men were inside, both bearded. The old man grinned at them. "Mark, Lou, meet Doc Feldman. Sit, Doc. I'm Jake Mullens, and you might say we were farmers."

The motor started with a wheeze. The tractor swung about and began heading away from Southport toward the desert dunes. It shook and rattled, but it seemed to make good time.

"I don't know anything about farming," Feldman protested.

Jake shrugged. "No, of course not. Couple of our friends heard about you where a spaceman was getting drunk and tipped us off. We know who you are. Here, try a bracky?"

Feldman took what seemed to be a cigarette and studied it doubtfully. It was coarse and fibrous inside, with a thin, hard shell that seemed to be a natural growth, as if it had been chopped from some vine. He lighted it, not knowing what to expect. Then he coughed as the bitter, rancid smoke burned at his throat. He started to throw it down, and hesitated. Jake was smoking one, and it had killed the craving for tobacco almost instantly.

"Some like 'em, most don't," Jake said. "They won't hurt you. Look—see that? Old Martian ruins. Built by some race a million years ago. Only half a dozen on Mars."

It was only a clump of weathered stone buildings in the light from the tractor, and Feldman had seen better in the stereo shots. It was interesting only because it connected with the legendary Martian race, like the canals that showed from space but could not be seen on the surface of the planet.

Feldman waited for the other to go on, but Jake was silent. Finally, he ground out the butt of the weed. "Okay, Jake. What do you want with me?"

"Consultation, maybe. Ever hear of herb doctors? I'm one of them."

Feldman knew that the Lobby permitted some leniency here, due to the scarcity of real medical help. There was only one decent hospital at Northport, on the opposite side of the planet.

Jake sighed and reached for another bracky weed. "Yeah, I'm pretty good with herbs. But I got a sick village on my hands and I can't handle it. We can't all mortgage our work to pay for a trip to Northport. Southport's all messed up while the new she-doctor gets her metabolism changed. Maybe the old guy there would have helped, but he died a couple months ago. So it looks like you're our only hope."

"Then you have no hope," Feldman told him sickly. "I'm a pariah, Jake. I can't do a thing for you."

"We heard about your argument with the Lobby. News reaches Mars. But these are mighty sick people, Doc."

Feldman shook his head. "Better take me back. I'm not allowed to practice medicine. The charge would be first-degree murder if anything happened."

Lou leaned forward. "Shall I talk to him, Jake?"

The old man grimaced. "Time enough. Let him see what we got first."

Sand howled against the windshield and the tractor bumped and surged along. Feldman took another of the weeds and tried to estimate their course. But he had no idea where they were when the tractor finally stopped. There was a village of small huts that seemed to be merely entrances to living quarters dug under the surface. They led him into one and through a tunnel into a large room filled with simple cots and the unhappy sounds of sick people.

Two women were disconsolately trying to attend to the half dozen sick—four children and two adults. Their faces brightened as they saw Jake, then fell. "Eb and Tilda died," they reported.

Feldman looked at the two figures under the sheets and whistled. The same black specks he had seen on the face of Billings covered the skins of the two old people who had died.

"Funny," Jake said slowly. "They didn't quite act like the

others and they sure died mighty fast. Darn it, I had it figured for that stuff in the book. Infantile paralysis. How about it, Doc? Sort of like a cold, stiff sore neck."

It was clearly polio—one of the diseases that could attack Mars-normal flesh. Feldman nodded at the symptoms, staring at the sick kids. He shrugged, finally. "There's a cure for it, but I don't have the serum. Neither do you, or you wouldn't have brought me here. I couldn't help if I wanted to."

"That old book didn't list a cure," Jake told him. "But it said the kids didn't have to be crippled. There was something about a Kenny treatment. Doc, does the stuff really cripple for life?"

Feldman saw one of the boys flinch. He dropped his eyes, remembering the Lobby's efficient spy service on Earth and wondering what it was like here. But he knew the outcome.

"Damn you, Jake!"

Jake chuckled. "Thought you would. We sure appreciate it. Just tell us what to do, Doc."

Feldman began writing down his requirements, trying to remember the details of the treatment. Exercise, hot compresses, massage. It was coming back to him. He'd have to do it himself, of course, to get the feel of it. He couldn't explain it well enough. But he couldn't turn his back on the kids, either.

"Maybe I can help," he said doubtfully as he moved toward a cot.

"No, Doc." Jake's voice wasn't amused any longer, and he held the younger man back. "You're doing us a favor, and I'll be darned if I'll let you stick your neck out too far. You can't treat 'em yourself. Mars is tougher than Earth. You should live under Space Lobby *and* Medical Lobby here a while. Oh, maybe they don't mind a few fools like me being herb doctors, but they'd sure hate to have a man who can do real medicine outside their hands. You let me do it, or get in the tractor and I'll have Lou drive you back. Once you start in here, there'll be no stopping. Believe me."

Feldman looked at him, seeing the colonials around him for the first time as people. It had been a long time since he'd been treated as a fellow human by anyone.

Jake was right, he knew. Once he put his hand to the bandage, eventually there'd be no turning back from the scalpel. These people needed medical help too desperately. Eventually, the news would spread, and the Lobby police would come for him. Chris couldn't afford to shield him. In fact, he was sure now that she'd hunt him night and day.

"Don't be a fool, Jake," he ordered brusquely. He handed his list to one of the women. "You'll have to learn to do what I do," he told the people there. "You'll have to work like fools for weeks. But there won't be many crippled children. I can promise that much!"

He blinked sharply at the sudden hope in their eyes. But his mind went on wondering how long it would be before the inevitable would catch up with him. With luck, maybe a few months. But he hadn't been blessed with any super-abundance of luck. It would probably be less time than he thought.

V

SURGERY

Doc Feldman's luck was better than he had expected. For an Earth year, he was a doctor again, moving about from village to village as he was needed and doing what he could.

The village had been isolated during the early colonization when Mars made a feeble attempt to break free of Space Lobby. Their supplies had been cut off and they had been forced to do for themselves. Now they were largely self-sufficient. They grew native plants and extracted hormones in crude little chemical plants. The hormones were traded to the big chemical plants for a pittance to buy what had to come from Earth. Other juryrigged affairs synthesized much of their food. But mostly they learned to get along on what Mars provided.

Doc Feldman learned from them. Money was no longer part of his life. He ate with whatever family needed him and slipped into the life around him.

He was learning Martian medicine and finding that his Earth courses were mostly useless. No wonder the villagers distrusted Lobby doctors. Doc had his own little laboratory where he had managed to start making Mars-normal penicillin—a primitive antibiotic, but better than nothing.

Jake had come to remind him that it was his first anniversary, and now they were smoking bracky together.

"Sheer luck, Jake," Doc repeated. "You Martians are tough. But some day someone is going to die under my care, with the little equipment I have. Then—"

Jake nodded slowly. "Maybe, Doc. And maybe some day Mars will break free of the Lobbies. You'd better pray for that."

"I've been—" Doc stopped, realizing what he'd started to say. The old man chuckled.

"You've been talking rebellion for months, Doc. I hear rumors. Whenever you get mad, you want us to secede. But you don't really mean it yet. You can't picture any government but the one you're used to."

Doc grinned. Jake had a point, but it was not as strong as it would have been a few months before. The towns under the Lobby were cheap imitations of Earth, but here, divorced to a large extent from the lobbies, the villages were making Mars their own. Their ways might be strange; but they worked.

Jake shifted his body in the weak sunlight. "Newton village forgot to report a death on time. I hear Ryan is sweating them out, trying to prove it was your fault."

There was no evidence against him yet, Doc was sure. But Chris was out to prove something, and to get a reputation as a top-flight administrator. It must have hurt when they shipped her here as head of the lesser hemisphere of Mars. She'd expected to use Feldman as a front while she became the actual ruler of the whole Lobby. Now she wanted to strike back.

"She's using blackmail," he said, and some of his old bitterness was in his voice. "Anyone taking treatment from an herb doctor in this section is cut off from Medical Lobby service. Damn it, Jake, that could mean letting people die!"

"Yeah." Jake sighed softly. "It could mean letting people begin to think about getting rid of the Lobby, too. Well, I gotta help harvest the bracky. Take it easy on operating for a while, will you, Doc?"

"All right, Jake. But stop keeping the serious cases a secret. Two men died last month because you wouldn't call me for surgery. I've broken all my oaths already. It doesn't matter anymore."

"It matters, boy. We've been lucky, but some day one case will go to the hospital and they'll find your former work. Then they'll really be after you. The less you do the better."

Doc watched Jake slump off, then turned down into the little root cellar and back toward the room concealed behind it, where his crude laboratory lay. For the moment, he was free to work on the mystery of the black spots.

He kept running into them—always on the body of someone who died of something that seemed like a normal disease. Without a microscope, he was almost helpless, but he had taken specimens and tried to culture them. Some of his cultures had grown, though they might be nothing but unknown Martian fungi or bacteria. Mars was dry and almost devoid of air, but plants and a few smaller insects had survived and adapted. It wasn't by any means lifeless.

Without a microscope, he could do little but depend on his files of cases. But today there was new evidence. A villager had filched an Earth *Medical Journal* from the tractor driven by Chris Ryan and forwarded it to him. He found the black specks mentioned in a single paragraph, under skin diseases. Investigation of the diet was being made, since all cases were among people eating synthetics.

There was another article on aberrant cases—a few strange little misbehaviors in classical syndromes. He studied that, wondering. It had to be the same thing. Diet didn't account for the fact that the specks appeared only when the patient was near death.

Nor did it account for the hard lump at the base of the neck which he found in every case he could check. That might be coincidence, but he doubted it.

Whatever it was, it aggravated any other disease the patient had and made seemingly simple diseases turn out to be completely and rapidly fatal. Once syphilis had been called "The Great Imitator". This gave promise of being worse.

He shook his head, cursing his lack of equipment. Each month more people were dying with these specks—and he was helpless.

The concealed door broke open suddenly and a boy thrust his head in. "Doc, there's a man here from Einstein. Says his wife's dying."

The man was already coming into the room.

"She's powerful sick, Doc. Had a bellyache, fever, began throwing up. Pains under her belly, like she's had before. But this time it's awful."

Doc shot a few questions at him, frowning at what he heard. Then he began packing the few things that might help. There should be no appendicitis on Mars. The bugs responsible for that shouldn't have adapted to Mars-normal. But more and more infections found ways to cross the border. Gangrene had been able to get by without change, it seemed. So far, none of the contagious infections except polio and the common cold had made the jump.

This sounded like an advanced case, perhaps already involving peritonitis.

So far, he'd been lucky with penicillin, but each time he used it with grave doubts of its action on the Mars-adapted patients. If the appendix had burst, however, it was the only possible treatment.

He riffled through his stores; There was ether enough,

fortunately. The villagers had made that for him out of Martian plants, using their complicated fermentation processes. He yelled for Jake, and the boy brought the old man back a moment later.

"Jake, I'll need more of that narcotic stuff. I don't want the woman writhing and tearing her stitches after the ether wears off."

"Can't get it, Doc." Jake's eyes seemed to cloud as he said it. "Distilling plant broke down. Doc, I don't like this case. That woman's been to the hospital three times. I hear she just got out recently. This might be a plant, or they figure they can't help her."

"They're afraid to try anything on Mars-normal flesh. They can't be proved wrong if they do nothing." Doc finished packing his bag and got ready to go out. "Jake, either I'm a doctor or I'm not. I can't worry when a woman may be dying."

For a second, Jake's expression was stubborn. Then the little crow's feet around his eyes deepened and the dry chuckle was back in his voice. "Right, Dr. Feldman." He flipped up his thumb and went off at a shuffling run toward the tractor. Lou and the man from Einstein followed Doc into the machine.

It was a silent ride, except for Doc's questions about the sick woman. Her husband, George Lynn, was evasive and probably ignorant. He admitted that Harriet had been to the dispensary and small infirmary that Southport called a hospital.

It was the only place in the entire Southern hemisphere where an operation could be performed legally. Most cases had to go to Northport, but Chris had been trying to expand. Apparently, she was determined to make Southport into another major center before she was called back to Earth.

Doc wondered why the villagers went there. They had no medical insurance with the Lobby; they couldn't afford it. Most villagers didn't have the cash, either. They were forced to mortgage their future work and that of their families to the drug plants that were run by the Lobby.

"And they just turned your wife away?" Doc asked. He couldn't quite believe that of Chris.

"Well, I dunno. She wouldn't talk much. Twice she went and they gave her something. Cost every cent I could borrow. Then this last time, they kept her a couple days before they let me come and get her. But now she's a lot worse."

Jake spun about, suddenly tense. "How'd you pay them last time, George?"

"Why, they didn't ask. I told her she could put up six months from me and the kids, but nobody said nothing about it. Just gave her back to me." He frowned slowly, his dull voice uncertain. "They told me they'd done all they could, not to bring her back. That's why she was so strong on getting Doc."

"I don't like it," Jake said flatly. "It stinks. They always charge. George, did they suggest she get in touch with Doc here?"

"Maybe they did, maybe not. Harriet did all the talking with them. I just do what she tells me, and she said to get Doc."

Jake swore. "It smells like a trap. Are you sure she's sick, George?"

"I felt her head and she sure had a fever." George Lynn was torn between his loyalties. "You know me, Doc. You fixed me up that time I had the red pip. I wouldn't pull nothing on you."

Doc had a feeling that Jake was probably right, but he vetoed the suggestion that they stop to look for spies. He had no time for that. If the woman was really sick, he had to get to her at once, and even that might be too late.

He remembered the woman, sickly from other treatment. He'd been forced to remove her inflamed tonsils a few months before. She'd whined and complained because he couldn't spend all his time attending her. She was a nag, a shrew, and a totally selfish woman. But that was her husband's worry, not his.

He dashed into the little house when they reached Einstein, and his first glance confirmed what George Lynn had said. The woman was sick, all right. She was running a high fever. Much too high.

She began whining and protesting at his having taken so long, but the pain soon forced her to stop.

"There may still be a chance," Doc told her husband brusquely. He threw the cleanest sheet onto a table and shoved it under the single light. "Keep out of the way—in the other room, if you can all pile in there. This isn't exactly aseptic, anyhow. You can boil a lot of water, if you want to help."

It would give them something to do and he could use the water to clean up. There was no time to wait for it, however. He had to sterilize with alcohol and carbolic acid, and hope. He bent over the woman, ripping her thin gown across to make room for the operation.

Then he swore.

Across her abdomen was the unhealed wound of a previous operation. They'd worked on her at Southport. They must have removed the appendix and then been shocked by the signs of infection. They weren't supposed to release a sick patient, but there was an easy out for them; they could remove her from the danger of spreading an unknown infection. Some doctors must have doped her up on sedatives and painkillers and sent her home, knowing that she would call him. For that matter, they might have noticed her unrecorded tonsillectomy and considered her fair bait.

He grabbed the ether and slapped a cone over her nose. She tried to protest; she never cooperated in anything. But the fumes of the ether he dipped onto the packing of the cone soon overcame that.

It was peritonitis, of course. The only thing to do was to go in and scrape and clean as best he could. It was a rotten job to have to do, and he should have had help. But he gritted his teeth and began. He couldn't trust anyone else to hold the instruments, even.

He cleaned the infection as best he could, knowing there was almost no chance. He used all the penicillin he dared. Then he began sewing up the incision. It was all he could do, except for dressing the wound with a sterile bandage. He reached for one, and stopped.

While he'd been working, the woman had died, far more quietly than she had ever lived.

It was probably the only gracious act of her life. But it was damning to Doc. They couldn't hide her death, and any investigation would show that someone had worked on her. To the Lobby, he would be the one who had murdered her.

Jake was waiting in the tractor. He took one look at Doc's face and made no inquiries.

They were more than a mile away when Jake pointed back. Small in the distance, but distinct against the sands, a gray Medical Corps tractor was coming. Either they'd had a spy in the village or they'd guessed the rate of her infection very closely. They must have hoped to catch Doc in the act, and they'd barely missed.

It wouldn't matter. Their pictures and what testimony they could force from the village should be enough to hang Doc.

VI

RESEARCH

There had been a council the night following the death of Harriet Lynn. Somehow the word had spread through the villages and the chiefs had assembled in Jake's village. But they had brought no solution, and in the long run had been forced to accept Doc's decision.

"I'm not going to retire and hide," he'd told them, surprised at his own decision, but grimly determined. "You need me and I need you. I'll move every day in hopes the Lobby police won't find me, but I won't quit."

Now he was packing the things he most needed and getting ready to move. The small bottles in which he was trying to grow his cultures would need warmth. He shoved them into an inner pocket, and began surveying what must be left.

He was heading for his tractor when another battered machine drove up. It had a girl of about fourteen, with tears streaming down her face. She held out a pleading hand, and her voice was scared. "It's—it's mama!"

"Where?"

"Leibnitz."

Leibnitz was near enough. Doc started his tractor, motioning for the girl to lead the way. The little dwelling she led him to was at the edge of the village, looking more poverty-stricken than most.

Chris Ryan, and three of the Medical Lobby police were

inside, waiting. The girl's mother was tied to the bed, with a collection of medical instruments laid out, but apparently the threat had been enough. No actual injury had been inflicted. Probably none had been intended seriously.

"I knew you'd answer that kind of call," Chris said coldly.

He grinned sickly. They'd wasted no time. "I hear it's more than you'll do, Chris. Congratulations! My patient died. You're lucky."

"She was certainly dead when my men took her picture. The print shows the death grimace clearly."

"Pretty. Frame it and keep it to comfort you when you feel lonely," he snapped.

She struck him across the mouth with the handle of her gun. Then she twisted out through the door quickly, heading for the tractor that had been camouflaged to look like those used by the villagers. The three police led him behind her.

A shout went up, and people began to rush onto the village street. But they were too late. By the time they reached Southport, Doc could see a trail of battered tractors behind, but there was nothing more the people could do. Chris had her evidence and her prisoner.

Judge Ben Wilson might have been Jake's brother. He was older and grayer, but the same expression lay on his face. He must have been the family black sheep, since his father had been president of Space Lobby. Instead of inheriting the position, Wilson had remained on Mars, safely out of the family's way.

He dropped the paper he was reading to frown at Chris. "This the fellow?"

She began formal charges, but he cut them off. "Your lawyer already had all that drawn up. I've been expecting you, Doctor. Doctor! Hnnf! You'd do a lot better home somewhere raising a flock of babies. Well, young fellow—so you're Feldman. Okay, your trial comes up day after tomorrow. Be a shame to lock you in Southport jail, a man of your importance. We'll just keep you here in the pending-trial room. It's a lot more comfortable."

Chris had been boiling slowly, and now she seemed to blow her safety valve. "Judge Wilson, your methods are your own business in local affairs. But this involves Earth Medical Lobby. I demand—"

"Tch, *tch!*" The judge stared at her reprovingly. "Young woman, you don't demand anything. This is Mars. If Space Lobby can stand me, I guess our friends over at Medical will have to. Or should I hold trial right now and find Feldman innocent for lack of evidence?"

"You wouldn't!" Chris cried. Then her face sobered suddenly. "I apologize. Medical is pleased to leave things in your hands, of course."

Wilson smiled. "Court's closed for today. Doc, I'll show you your cell. It's right next to my study, so I'm heading there anyhow."

He began shucking his robe while Chris went out with the police, her voice sharp and continual.

The cell was both reasonably escape-proof and comfortable, Doc saw, and he tried to thank the judge.

But the old man waved it aside. "Forget it. I just like to see that little termagant taken down. But don't count on my being soft. My methods may be a bit unusual—I always did like the courtroom scenes in the old books by that fellow Smith—but Space Lobby never had any reason to reverse my decisions. Anything you need?"

"Sure," Doc told him, grinning in spite of his bitterness. "A good biology lab and an electron microscope."

"Umm. How about a good optical mike and some

stains? Just got them in on the last shipment. Figure they were meant for you anyhow, since Jake Mullens asked me to order them."

He went out and came back with the box almost at once. He snorted at Doc's incredulous thanks and moved off, his bedroom slippers slapping against the hard floor.

Doc stared after him. If he were a friend of Jake, willing to invent some excuse to get a microscope here . . . but it didn't matter. Friend or foe, his death sentence would be equally fatal. And there were other things to be thought of now. The little microscope was an excellent one, though only a monocular.

Doc's hands trembled as he drew his cultures out and began making up a slide. The sun offered the best source of light near the window, and he adjusted the instrument. Something began to come into view, but too faintly to be really visible.

He remembered the stains, trying to recall his biology courses. More by luck than skill, his fourth try gave him results.

Under two thousand powers, he could just see details. There were dozens of cells in his impure culture, but only one seemed unfamiliar. It was a long, worm-like thing, sharpened at both ends, with the three separate nuclei that were typical of Martian life forms. Nearby were a host of little rodlike squiggles just too small to see clearly.

Martian life! No Martian bug had ever proved harmful to men. Yet this was no mutated cell or virus from Earth; it was a new disease, completely different from all others. It was one where all Earth's centuries of experience with bacteria would be valueless—the first Martian disease. Unless this was simply some accidental contamination of his culture, not common to the other samples. He worked on until the light was too faint before putting the microscope aside.

By the time the trial commenced, however, he was sure of the cause of the disease. It *was* Martian. Crude as his cultures were, they had proved that.

The little courtroom was filled, mostly from the villages. Lou was there, along with others he had come to know. Then the sight of Jake caught Doc's eyes. The darned fool had no business there; he could get too closely mixed into the whole mess.

"Court's in session," Wilson announced. "Doc, you represented by counsel?"

Jake's voice answered. "Your Honor, I represent the defendant. I think you'll find my credentials in order."

Chris started to protest, but Wilson grinned. "Never lost your standing in spite of that little fracas thirty years ago, so far as I know. But the police thought you were a witness when you came walking in. Figured you were giving up."

"I never said so," Jake answered.

Chris was squirming angrily, but the florid man acting as counsel for Medical Lobby shook his head, bending over to whisper in her ear. He straightened. "No objection to counsel for the defense. We recognize his credentials."

"You're a fool, Matthews," the judge told him. "Jake was smarter than half the rest of Legal Lobby before he went native. Still can tie your tail to a can. Okay, let's start things. I'm too old to dawdle."

Doc lost track of most of what happened. This was totally unlike anything on Earth, though it might have been in keeping with the general casualness of the villages. Maybe the ritualistic routine of the Lobbies was driving those who could resist to the opposite extreme.

Chris was the final witness. Matthews drew comment of Feldman's former crime from her, and Jake made no protest, though Wilson seemed to expect one. Then she began sewing his shroud. There wasn't a fact that managed to emerge without slanting, though technically correct. Jake sat quietly, smiling faintly, and making no protests.

He got up lazily to cross-examine Chris. "Dr. Ryan, when Daniel Feldman was examined by the Captain of the *Navaho* after arriving at Mars station, did you identify him then as having been Dr. Daniel Feldman?"

She glanced at Matthews, who seemed puzzled but unconcerned. "That's correct," she admitted. "But—"

"And you later saw him delivered to the surface of Mars. Is that also correct?" When she assented, Jake hesitated. Then he frowned. "What did you do then? Did you report him or send anyone to look after him or anything like that?"

"Certainly not," she answered. "He was no—"

"You did absolutely nothing about him after you identified him and saw him delivered here? You're quite sure of that?"

"I did nothing."

Jake stood quietly for a moment, then shrugged. "No more questions."

Matthews finished things in a plea for the salvation of all humanity from the danger of such men as Daniel Feldman. He was looking smug, as was Chris.

Wilson turned to Jake. "Has the defense anything to say?"

"A few things, Your Honor." Jake stood up, suddenly looking certain and pleased. "We are happy to admit everything factual the Lobby had testified. Daniel Feldman performed a surgical operation on Harriet Lynn in the village of Einstein. But when has it been illegal for a member of the Medical profession to perform an operation, even with small chance of success, within an accepted area for such operation? There has been no evidence adduced that any crime or act of even unethical conduct was committed."

That brought Chris and Matthews to their feet. Wilson

was relaxed again, looking as if he'd swallowed a whole cage of canaries. He banged his gavel down.

Jake picked up two ragged and dog-eared volumes from his table. "Case of Harding vs. Southport, 2043, establishes that a Lobby is responsible for any member on Mars. It is also responsible for informing the authorities of any criminal conduct on the part of its members or any former member known to it. Failure to report shall be considered an admission that the Lobby recognizes the member as one in good standing and accepts responsibility for that member's conduct.

"At the time Daniel Feldman arrived, Dr. Christina Ryan was the highest appointed representative of Medical Lobby in Southport, with full authority. She identified Feldman as having been a doctor, without stipulating any change in status. She made no further report to any authority concerning Daniel Feldman's presence here. It seems obvious that Medical Lobby at Southport thereby accepted Daniel Feldman as a doctor in good standing for whose conduct the Lobby accepted full responsibility."

Wilson studied the book Jake held out, and nodded. "Seems pretty clear-cut to me," he agreed, passing the book on to Matthews. "There's still the charge that Dr. Feldman operated outside a hospital."

"No reason he shouldn't," Jake said. He handed over the other volume. "This is the charter for Medical Lobby on Mars. Medical Lobby agrees to perform all necessary surgical and medical services for the planet, though at the signing of this charter there was no hospital on Mars. Necessarily, Medical Lobby agreed to perform surgery outside of any hospital, then. But to make it plainer, there's a later paragraph—page 181—that defines each hospital zone as extending not less than three nor more than one hundred miles. Einstein is about one hundred and ten miles from the nearest hospital at Southport, so Einstein comes under the original charter provisions. Dr. Feldman was forced by charter provisions to protect the good name of his Lobby by undertaking any necessary surgery in Einstein."

He waited until Matthews had scanned that book, then took it back and began packing a big bag. Doc saw that his possessions and the microscope were already in the bag. The old man paid no attention to the arguments of Matthews before the bench.

Abruptly Wilson pounded his gavel. "This court finds that Dr. Daniel Feldman is qualified to practice all the arts and skills of the medical profession on Mars and that he acted ethically in the performance of his duties in the case of the deceased Harriet Lynn," he ruled. "The costs of the case shall be billed to Medical Lobby of Southport."

He took off his robe and moved rapidly toward his private quarters. Court was closed.

Doc got up shakily, not daring to believe fully what he had heard. He started toward Jake, trying to avoid bumping into Chris. But she would not be avoided. She stood in front of him, screaming accusations and threats that reminded him of the only fight they'd ever had during their brief marriage.

When she ran down, he finally met her eyes. "You're a helluva doctor," he told her harshly. "You spend all your time fighting me when there's a plague out there that may be worse than any disease we've ever known. Take a look at what lies under the black specks on your corpses. You'll find the first Martian disease. And maybe if you begin working on that now, you can learn to be a real doctor in time to do something about it. But I doubt it."

She fell back from him then. "Research! You've been doing unauthorized research!"

"Prove it," he suggested. "But you'd be a lot smarter to try some yourself, and to hell with your precious rules."

He followed Jake out to the tractor.

Surprisingly, the old man was sweating now. He shook his head at Doc's look, and his grin was uncertain.

"Matthews is an incompetent," he said. "They could have had you, Doc. That charter is so sloppy a man can prove anything by it, and building a hospital here did bring in Earth rules. Wilson went out on a limb in letting you go. But I guess we got away with it. Let's get out of here."

Doc climbed into the tractor more soberly. They had escaped this time. But there would be another time, and he was pretty sure that would be Chris' round. He had no intention of giving up his research.

VII

PLAGUE

Dr. Feldman leaned back from his microscope and lighted another bracky weed. He glanced about the room and sighed wearily. Maybe he'd been better off when he had no friends and couldn't risk the safety of others in an effort to do research that was the highest crime on two worlds.

The evidence of his work was hidden thirty feet beyond his former laboratory in Jake's village, with a tunnel that led from another root-cellar. The theory was the old one that the best place to avoid discovery was where you had already been discovered. If their spies had identified his former hangout, they'd never expect to have him set up research nearby. It was a nice theory, but he wasn't sure of it.

Jake looked up from a cot where he'd been watching the improvised culture incubator. "Stop tearing yourself to bits, Doc. We know the danger and we're still darned glad to have you here working on this."

"I'm trying to put myself together into a whole man," Doc told him. "But I seem to come out wholly a fool."

"Yeah, sure. Sometimes it takes a fool to get things done; wise men wait too long for the right time. How's the bug hunt?"

Doc grunted in disgust and swung back to the microscope. Then he gave up as his tired eyes refused to focus. "Why don't you people revolt?"

"They tried it twice. But they were just a bunch of pariahs shipped here to live in peonage. They couldn't do much. The first time Earth cut off shipments and starved them. Next time the villages had the answer to that but the cities had to fight for Earth or starve, so they whipped us. And there's always the threat that Earth could send over unmanned war rockets loaded with fissionables."

"So it's hopeless?"

"So nothing! The Lobbies are poisoning themselves, like cutting off Medical service until they cut themselves out of a job. It's just a matter of time. Go back to the bugs, Doc."

Doc sighed and reached for his notes. "I wish I knew more Martian history. I've been wondering whether this bug may not have been what killed off the old Martians. Something had to do it, the way they disappeared. I wish I knew enough to make an investigation of those ruins out there."

"Durwood!" Jake had propped himself on an elbow, staring at Doc in surprise.

Doc scowled. "Clive Durwood, you mean? The archeologist who dug up what little we know about the ruins?"

"Yeah, before he went back to Earth and started living off his lectures. He came here again three years ago and dropped dead in Edison on the way to some other ruins. Heart failure, they called it, though it was more like the two old farmers who ran themselves to death last month. I saw him when they buried him. His face looked funny, and I think he had those little specks, though I may remember wrong." He grimaced. "Mars is tough, Doc; it has to be. Some of the plant seeds Durwood found in the ruins grew! Maybe your bugs waited a million years till we came along."

"What about the farmers? Did they meet Durwood?"

Jake nodded. "Must have. He lived in their village most of the time."

Doc went through his notes. He'd asked for reports on all deaths, and he finally found the account. The two old men had been nervous and fidgety for weeks. They were twins, living by themselves, and nobody paid much attention. Then one morning both were seen running wildly in circles. The village managed to tie them up, but they died of exhaustion shortly after.

It wasn't a pretty picture. The disease might have an incubation period of nearly fifteen years, judging by the length of time it had taken to hit Durwood. It must spread from person to person during an early contagious stage, leaving widening circles behind Durwood and those first infected. When matured, any other sickness would set it off, with few symptoms of its own. But without help, it still killed its victims, apparently driving them madly toward frenzied physical effort.

He studied the culture on a slide again. He'd tried Koch's method to get a pure strain, splattering the bugs onto a native starchy root and plucking off individual colonies. About twenty specimens had been treated with every chemical he could find. So far he'd found a few things that seemed to stop their growth, but nothing that killed them, except stuff far too harsh to use in living tissue.

He had nearly forty cases of deaths that showed symptoms now, and he went back over them, looking for anything in common that went back ten to twenty years before death. There were no rashes nor blisters. A few had had apparent colds, but such were too common to mean anything.

Only one thing appeared, about fourteen years before their deaths. The people interviewed about the victims might be vague about most things, but they remembered the time when "Jim had the jumping headache."

"Jake," Doc called, "what's jumping headache? Most people seem to have it some time or other, but I haven't run across a case of it."

"Sure you have, Doc. Mamie Brander's little girl a few weeks ago. Feels like your pulse is going to rip your skull off, right here. Can't eat because chewing drives you crazy. Back of your head, neck and shoulders swell up for about a week. Then it goes away."

Then it goes away—for fourteen years, until it comes back to kill!

Doc stared at his charts in sudden horror. It was a new disease—thought to be some virus, but not considered dangerous. Selznik's migraine, according to medical usage; you treated it with hot pads and anodyne, and it went away easily enough.

He'd seen hundreds of such cases on Earth. There must be millions who had been hit by it. The patent-medicine branch of the Lobby had even brought out something called Nograine to use for self-treatment.

"Something important?" Jake wanted to know.

Feldman nodded. "How much weight do you swing in other villages, Jake?"

"People sort of do me favors when I ask," Jake admitted. "Like swiping those medical journals from Northport for you, or like Molly Badger getting that job as maid to spy on Chris Ryan. Name it and I'll do my best."

Doc had a vague idea of village politics, but he had more important things to think of. Most of his foul mood had disappeared with the clue he'd stumbled on, and his chief worry now was to clinch the facts.

Feldman considered the problem. "I want a report on every case of jumping headache in every village—who had it, when, and how old they were. This place first, but every village you can reach. And I'll want someone to take a letter to Chris Ryan."

Jake frowned at that, but went out to issue instructions. Doc sat down at a battered old typewriter. Writing Chris might do no good, but some warning had to be gotten through to Earth, where the vast resources of Medical Lobby could be thrown into the task of finding the cause and cure of the disease. The connection with Selznik's migraine had to be reported. If something could blast the Lobby into action, it wouldn't matter quite so much what they did to him. He wasn't foolish enough to expect gratitude from them, but he was getting used to the idea that his days were numbered. The plague was more important than what happened to him.

The letter had been dispatched by the time Jake returned. "Here's the dope for this village. Everybody accounted for except you."

"Never had it, Jake." Feldman went down the list. "Most of it fourteen years ago. That fits. About the only exceptions are the kids who seem to get it between the ages of two and three. Eighty-seven out of ninety-one!"

He stared at the figures sickly. Most of the village not only had the plague but must be near the end of the incubation period. It looked as if most of the village would be dead before another year passed.

"Bad?" Jake asked.

"The first symptom of Martian fever."

The old man whistled, the lines around his eyes tightening. "Must be me," he decided. "I'm the guy who must have brought it here, then. I used to spend a lot of time with Durwood at his diggings!"

There was a constant commotion all that day and the next as runners went out to the villages and came back with reports. The variation from village to village was only slight. Most of Mars seemed to have advanced cases of Martian fever.

Without animals for investigation and study, real research was difficult. Doc also needed an electron microscope. He was reasonably sure that the disease must travel through the nerves, but he had found no proof beyond the hard lump at the base of the neck. There it was a fair-sized organism. Elsewhere he could find nothing, until the black specks developed.

His eyes ached from trying to see more than was visible in the microscope. The tantalizing suggestions of filaments around the nuclei might be the form of plague that was contagious. They might even be the true form of the bug, with the bigger cell only a transition stage. There were a number of diseases that involved complicated changes in the organisms that caused them. But he couldn't be sure.

He finally buried his head in his hands, trying to do by pure thought what he couldn't do in any other way. And even there, he lacked training. He was a doctor, not a xenobiologist. Research training had been taboo in school, except for a favored few.

The reports continued to come in, confirming the danger. They seemed to have the worst plague on their hands in all human history; and nobody who could do anything about it even knew of it.

"Molly reports that your letter got some results," Jake reported. "Chris Ryan brought home one of the electron microscopes and a bunch of equipment from the hospital pathology room. Think she'll get anywhere?"

Doc doubted it. Damn it, he hadn't meant for her to try it, though she might have authority for routine experiments. But it was like her to refuse to pass on the word without trying to prove her own suspicion of him first.

He tried to comfort himself with the fact that some men were immune, or seemed so; about three out of a hundred showed no signs. If that immunity was hereditary, it might save the race. If not. . . .

Jake came in at twilight with a grim face. "More news from Molly. The Lobby is starting out to comb every village with a fault-finder, starting here. And this hole will show up like a sore thumb. Better start packing. We gotta be out of here in less than an hour!"

VIII

FOOL

Three days later, Doc saw his first runner.

The tractor was churning through the sand just before sundown, heading toward another one-night stand at a new village. Lou was driving, while Doc and Jake brooded silently in the back, paying no attention to the colors that were blazoned over the dunes. The cat-and-mouse game was getting to Doc. There was no real assurance that the village they were approaching might not be the target the Lobby had chosen for the next investigation.

Lou braked the tractor to a sudden halt, and pointed.

A figure was running frantically over one of the low dunes with the little red sun behind him. He seemed headed toward them, but as he drew nearer they could see that he had no definite direction. He simply ran, pumping his legs frantically as if all the devils of hell were after him. His body swayed from side to side in exhaustion, but his arms and legs pumped on.

"Stop him!" Jake ordered, and Lou swung the tractor. It halted squarely in the runner's path, and the figure struck against it and toppled.

The legs went on pumping, digging into the dirt and gravel, but the man was too far gone to rise. Jake and Lou shoved him through the doors into the tractor and Doc yanked off his aspirator.

The man was giving vent to a kind of ululating cry, weakened now almost to a whine that rose and fell with the motion of his legs. Sweat had once streaked his haggard face, but it was dry and blanched to a pasty gray.

Doc injected enough narcotic to quiet a maddened bull. It had no effect, except to upset the rhythm of the arms and legs. It took five more minutes for the man to die.

The specks were larger this time—the size of periods in twelve-point type. The lump at the base of the skull was as big as a small hen's egg.

"From Edison, like the others so far. Jack Kooley," Jake answered Doc's question. "Durwood spent a lot of time here on his first expedition, so it's getting the worst of it."

Doc pulled the aspirator mask back over the man's face and they carried him out and laid him on a low dune. They couldn't risk returning the corpse to its people.

This was only the primary circle of infection, direct from Durwood. The second circle could be ten times as large, as the infection spread from one to a few to many. So far it was localized. But it wouldn't stay that way.

Doc climbed slowly out of the tractor, lugging his small supplies of equipment, while Jake made arrangements for them to spend the night in a deserted house. But the figure of the runner and his own failures to find more about the disease kept haunting Doc. He began setting up his equipment grimly.

"Better get some sleep," Jake suggested. "You're a mite more tired than you think. Anyhow, I thought you told me you couldn't do any more with what you've got."

Feldman looked at the supplies he had spread out, and shook his head wearily. He'd been over every chemical and combination a dozen times, without results that showed in the limited magnification of the optical mike.

He snapped the case shut and hit the rude table with the

heel of his hand. "There are other supplies. Jake, do you have any signal to get in touch with Molly at the Ryan house?"

"Three raps on the rear left window. I'll get Lou."

"No!" Doc came to his feet, reaching for his jacket. "They're looking for three men now. It's safer if I go alone—and I'm the only one who knows what supplies are needed. With luck, I may even get the electron mike. Got a gun I can borrow?"

Jake found one somewhere, an old revolver with a few loads. He began protesting, but Doc overruled him sharply. Three men could no more fight off the police than one, if they were spotted. He swung toward the tractor.

"You'd better start spreading the word on everything we know. If people realize they're already safe or doomed it'll be better than having them going crazy to avoid contagion."

"Most of the villages know already," Jake told him. "And damn it, get back here, Doc. If you can't make it, turn tail quick, and we'll think of something else."

Southport seemed normal enough as Doc drove through its streets. The stereo house was open, and the little shops were brightly lighted. He stopped once to pull a copy of Southport's little newspaper from a dispenser. All was quiet on its front page, too.

As usual, though, the facts were buried inside. The editorial was pouring too much oil on the waters in its lauding of the role of Medical Lobby on Mars for no apparent reason. The death notices no longer listed the cause of death. Medical knew something was up, at least, and was worried.

He parked the tractor behind Chris' house and slipped to the proper window. Everything was seemingly quiet there. At his knock, the shade was drawn back, and he caught a brief glimpse of Molly looking out. A moment later she opened the rear lock to let him into the kitchen.

"Shh. She's still up, I think. What can I do, Doc?"

He tried to smile at her. "Hide me until it's safe to get into her laboratory. I've got to—"

The inner kitchen was kicked open and Chris stood beyond it, holding a cocked gun in her hand.

"It took longer than I expected, Dan," she said quietly. "But after your letter, I knew you'd swallow the bait. You bloody fool! Did you really believe I'd start doing research here just because of your imaginings?"

He slumped slowly back against the sink. "So this is a fool's errand, then? There never was any equipment here?"

"The equipment's here—in my office. I guessed your spies would report it, so it had to be here. But it won't help you now, pariah Feldman!"

He came from his braced position against the sink like a spring uncoiling. He expected her to shoot, but hoped the surprise would ruin her aim. Then it was too late, and his boot hit the gun savagely, knocking it from her hand. Life in the villages had hardened him surprisingly. She was comparatively helpless in his hands. A few minutes later, he had her bound securely with surgical tape Molly brought him. She raged furiously in the chair where he'd dumped her, then gave up.

"They'll get you, Daniel Feldman!" Surprisingly, there was no rage in her voice now. "You won't get away from us. The planet isn't big enough."

"I got away from your trial," he reminded her. "And I got away and lived when you left me without a chance on the ground of the spaceport."

She laughed harshly. "*You* got away then? You fool, who do you think gave you the extra battery so you could live long enough to be helped at the spaceport? Who hired a fool like Matthews so you wouldn't get the death sentence you deserved? Who let you get away as an herb doctor for months before you set yourself up as God and a traitor to mankind again?"

It shook him, as it was probably intended to do. How had she known about the extra battery? He'd always assumed that Ben had returned to give it to him. But in that case, Chris couldn't know of it. Then he hardened himself again. In the old days, she'd always had one trump card he couldn't beat and hadn't expected. But too much was involved for games now.

"Any police around, Molly?" he asked.

Molly came back a minute later to report that everything looked clear and to show him where the equipment had been set up in Chris' office. It was all there, including the electron mike—a beautiful little portable model. There was even a small incubator with its own heat source into which he immediately transferred the little bottles he'd been keeping warm against his skin. Most of the equipment had never been unpacked, which made loading it onto his tractor ridiculously easy.

"Better come with me now, Molly," he suggested at last. Then he turned to Chris, who was watching him with almost no expression. "You can wriggle your chair to the phone in half an hour, I guess. Knock the phone off and yell for help. It's better than you deserve, unless you really did leave me that battery."

"You won't get away with it," she told him again, calmly this time.

"No," he admitted. "Probably not. But maybe the human race will, if I have time to find an answer to the plague you won't see under your nose. But you won't get away with it, either. In the long run, your kind never do."

Molly was sniffling as they drove away. It had probably been the best life she'd known, Doc supposed. Chris could be kind to menials. But now Molly's work was done, and she'd have to disappear into the villages. He let her off at the first village and drove on alone. He was itching to get to the microscope now, hardly able to wait through the long journey back to Jake. His impatience grew with each mile.

Finally he gave up. He swung the tractor into a small gulley between sand dunes, left the motor idling and pulled down the shades the villagers used for blackout traveling. There was power enough for the mike here, and the cab was big enough for what he had to do.

He mounted the mike on the tractor seat and began laying out the collection of smears and cultures he had brought. It had been years since he'd made a film for the electron mike, but he found it all came back to him as he worked.

His hands were sweating with tension as he inserted the first film into the chamber. He had the magnetic "lenses" set for twenty thousand power, but a quick glance showed it was too weak. He raised the power to fifty thousand.

The filaments were there, clear and distinct.

He turned on the little tape recorder that had been part of Chris' equipment and set the microphone where he could dictate into it without stopping to make clumsy notes. He readjusted the focus carefully, carrying on a running commentary.

Then he gasped. Each of the little filaments carried three tiny darker sections; each was a cell, complete in itself, with the typical Martian triple nucleus.

He put a film with a tiny section of the nerve tissue from a corpse into the chamber next, and again a quick glance at the screen was enough. The filaments were there, thickly crowded among nerve cells. They *did* travel along the nerves to reach the base of the brain before the larger lump could form.

A specimen from one of the black specks was even more

interesting. The filaments were there, but some were changed or changing into tiny, round cells, also with the triple dark spots of nuclei. Those must be the final form that was released to infect others. Probably at first these multiplied directly in epithelial tissue, so that there was a rapid contagion of infection. Eventually, they must form the filaments that invaded the nerves and caused the brief bodily reaction that was Selznik's migraine. Then the body adapted to them and they began to incubate slowly, developing into the large cells he had first seen. When "ripe", the big cells broke apart into millions of the tiny round ones that went back to the nerve endings, causing the black spots and killing the host.

He knew his enemy now, at least.

He reached for the controls, increasing the magnification. He would lose resolution, but he might find something more at the extreme limits of the mike.

Something wet and cold gushed into his face. He jerked back, trying to wipe it off, but it was already evaporating, and there was a thick, acrid odor in the cab. He grabbed for his aspirator, then tried to reach the airlock. But paralysis was already spreading through him, and he toppled to the floor before he could escape.

When he came to, it was morning outside, and Chris was waiting inside the cab with two big Lobby policemen. A hypo in her hand must have been what revived him.

She touched the electron microscope with something like affection. "The Lobby technicians did a good job on this, don't you think, Dan? I warned you, but you wouldn't listen. And now we've even got your own taped words to prove you were doing forbidden research. Fool!"

She shook her head pityingly as the tractor began moving with two others toward Southport.

"You and your phony diseases. A little skin disorder,

Selznik's migraine, and a few cases of psychosis to make a new disease. Do you think Medical Lobby can't check on such simple things? Or didn't you expect us to hear of your open talk of revolt and realize you were planning to create some new germ to wipe out the Earth forces. Maybe those runners of yours were real, mass murderer!"

She drew out another hypo and shoved the needle into his arm. Necrosynth—enough to keep him unconscious for twenty-four hours. He started to curse her, but the drug acted before he could complete the thought.

IX

JUDGMENT

Doc woke to see sunlight shining through a heavily barred window that must be in the official Southport jail. He waited a few minutes for his head to clear and then sat up; necrosynth left no hangover, at least.

The sound of steps outside was followed by the squeak of a key in the lock. "Fifteen minutes, Judge Wilson," a voice said.

"Thank you, officer." Wilson came into the cell, carrying a tray of breakfast and a copy of the Northport *Gazette*. He began unloading bracky weeds from his pocket while Doc attacked the breakfast.

"They tossed the book at you, Doc," he said. "You haven't got a chance, and there's nothing the villages can do. Trial's set for tomorrow at Northport, and it's in closed session. We can't get you off this time."

Doc nodded. "Thanks for coming, even if there's nothing you can do. I've been living on borrowed time for a year, anyhow, so I have no right to kick. But who's 'we'?"

"The villages. I've been part of their organization for years." The old man sighed heavily. "You might say a revolution has been going on since I can remember, though most villagers don't know it. We've just been waiting our time. Now we've stopped waiting and the rifles will be coming out—rifles made in village shops. The villages are going to rebel, even if we're all dead of plague in a month."

Doc Feldman nodded and reached for the bracky. He knew that this was their way of trying to make him feel his work hadn't been for nothing, and he was grateful for Wilson's visit. "It was a good year for me. Damned good. But time's running short. I'd better brief you on the latest on the plague."

Wilson began making notes until Doc was finished. Finally he got up as steps sounded from the hall. "Anything else?"

"Just a guess. A lot of Earth germs can't live in Mars-normal flesh; maybe this can't live in Earth-normal. Tell them so long for me."

"So long, Doc." He shook hands briefly and was waiting at the door when the guard opened it.

An hour later, the Lobby police took Feldman to the Northport shuttle rocket. They had some trouble on the way; a runner cut down the street, with the crowds frantically rushing out of his way. Terror was reaching the cities already.

Doc flashed a look at Chris. "Mob hysteria. Like flying saucers and wriggly tops, I suppose?" he asked, before the guard could stop him.

They locked his legs, but left his hands free in the rocket. He unfolded the paper Wilson had brought and buried his face in it. Then he swore. They *were* explaining the runners as a case of mob hysteria!

Northport was calmer. Apparently they had yet to have first-hand experience with the plague. But now nothing seemed quite real to Doc, even when they locked him into the big Northport jail. The whole ritual of the Lobbies seemed like a fantasy after the villages.

It snapped back into focus, however, when they led him

into the trial room of the Medical Lobby building. It was a smaller version of his trial on Earth. Fear washed in by association. The complete lack of humanity in the procedure was something from a half-remembered and horrible past.

The presiding officer asked the routine question: "Is the prisoner represented by counsel?"

Blane, the dapper little prosecutor, arose quickly. "The prisoner is a pariah, Sir Magistrate."

"Very well. The court will accept the protective function for the prisoner. You may proceed."

I'll be judge, I'll be jury. And prosecution and defense. It made for a lot less trouble. Of course, if Space Lobby had asserted interest, it would have gone to a supposedly neutral court. But as usual, Space was happy to leave it in the hands of Medical.

The tape was played as evidence. Doc frowned. The words were his, but there had been a lot of editing that subtly changed the import of his notes.

"I protest," he challenged. "It's not an accurate version."

The Lobby magistrate turned a wooden face to him. "Does the prisoner have a different version to introduce?"

"No, but—"

"The evidence is accepted. One of the prisoner's six protests will be charged against him."

Blane smiled smoothly and held up a small package. "We wish to introduce this drug as evidence that the prisoner is a confirmed addict, morally irresponsible under addiction. This is a package of so-called bracky weed, a vile and noxious substance found in his possession."

"It has alkaloids no more harmful than nicotine," Feldman stated sharply.

"Do you contend that you find the taste pleasing?" Blane asked.

"It's bitter, but I've gotten used to it."

"I've tasted it," the magistrate said. "Evidence accepted. Two deductions, one for irregularity of presentation."

Doc shrugged and sat back. He'd tested his rights and found what he expected. It was hard to see now how he had ever accepted such procedure. Jake must be right; they'd been in power too long, and were making the mistake of taking the velvet glove off the iron fist and flailing about for the sheer pleasure of power.

It dragged on, while he became a greater and greater monster on the record. But finally it was over, and the magistrate turned to Feldman. "You may present your defense."

"I ask complete freedom of expression," Doc said formally.

The magistrate nodded. "This is a closed court. Permission granted. The recording will be scrambled."

The last bit ruined most of the purpose Doc had in mind. But it was too late to change. He could only hope that some one of the Medical men present would remember something of what he said.

"I have nothing to say for myself," he began. "It would be useless. But I had to do what I did. There's a plague outside. I've studied that plague, and I have knowledge which must be used against it. . . ."

He sat down in three minutes. It had been useless.

Blane arose, with a smile still plastered on his face. "We, of course, recognize the existence of a new contagion, but I believe we have established that this is one disseminated by the prisoner himself, and probably not directly contagious. There have been many cases of fanatics ready to destroy humanity to eliminate those they hate. Now, surely, the prisoner has himself left no question of his attitude. He asserts he has knowledge and skill greater than the entire Medical Research staff. He has attempted to intimidate us by threats.

He is clearly psychopathic, and dangerously so. The prosecution rests."

The guards took Doc into the anteroom, where he was supposed to hear nothing that went on. But their curiosity was stronger than their discretion, and the door remained a trifle ajar.

The magistrate began the discussion. "The case seems firm enough. It's fortunate Dr. Ryan acted so quickly, with some of the people getting nervous. Perhaps it might be wise to publicize our verdict."

"My thought exactly," Blane agreed. "If we show Feldman is responsible and that Medical is eliminating the source of the infection, it may have a stabilizing effect."

"Let's hope so. The sentence will have to be death, of course. We can't let such a rebellious psychopath live. But this needs something more, it seems. You've prepared a recommendation, I suppose."

"There was the case of Albrecht Delier," Blane suggested. "Something like that should have good publicity impact."

It struck Doc that they sounded as if they believed themselves—as the witch-burners had believed in witches. He was sweating when the guards led him before the bench.

The magistrate rolled a pen slowly across his fingers as his eyes raked Feldman. "Pariah Daniel Feldman, you have been found guilty on all counts. Furthermore, your guilt must be shared by that entire section of Mars known as the villages. Therefore the entire section shall be banned and forbidden any and all services of the Medical Lobby for a period of one year."

"Sir Magistrate!" One of the members of Southport Hospital staff was on his feet. "Sir Magistrate, we can't cut them off completely."

"We must, Dr. Harkness. I appreciate the fine humanitarian tradition of our Lobby which lies behind your protest, but at such a time as this the good of the body politic requires drastic measures. Why not see me after court, and we can discuss it then?"

He turned back to Feldman, and his face was severe.

"The same education which has produced such fine young men as Dr. Harkness was wasted on you and perverted to endanger the whole race. No punishment can equal your crimes, but there is one previously invoked for a particularly horrible case, and it seems fitting that you should be the fourth so sentenced.

"Daniel Feldman, you are sentenced to be taken in to space beyond planetary limits, together with all material used by you in the furtherance of your criminal acts. There you shall be placed into a spacesuit containing sufficient oxygen for one hour of life, and no more. You and your contaminated possessions shall then be released into space, to drift there through all eternity as a warning to other men.

"This sentence shall be executed at the earliest possible moment, and Dr. Christina Ryan is hereby commissioned to observe such execution. And may God have mercy on your soul!"

X

EXECUTION

The hours of waiting were blurred for Doc. There were periods when fear clogged his throat and left him gasping with the need to scream and beat his cell walls. There were also times when it didn't seem to matter, and when his only thoughts were for the villages and the plague.

They brought him the papers, where he was painted as a monster beside whom Jack the Ripper and Albrecht Delier were gentle amateurs. They were trying to focus all fear and resentment on him. Maybe it was working. There were screaming crowds outside the jail, and the noise of their hatred was strong enough to carry through even the atmosphere of Mars. But there were also signs that the Lobby was worried, as if afraid that some attempt might still be made to rescue him.

He'd looked forward to the trip to the airport as a way of judging public reaction. But apparently the Lobby had no desire to test that. The guards led him up to the roof of the jail, where a rocket was waiting. The landing space was too small for one of the station shuttles, but a little Northport-Southport shuttle was parked there after what must have been a difficult set-down. The guards tested Doc's manacles and forced him into the shuttle.

Inside, Chris was waiting, carrying an official automatic. There was also a young pilot, looking nervous and unhappy. He was muttering under his breath as the guards locked Doc's legs to a seat and left.

"All right," Chris ordered. "Up ship!"

"I tell you we're overweight with you. I wasn't counting on three for the trip," the pilot protested. "The only thing that will get this into orbit with the station is faith. I'm loaded with every drop of fuel she'll hold and it still isn't enough."

"That's your problem," Chris told him firmly. "You've got your orders, and so have I. Up ship!"

If she had her own worries about the shuttle, she didn't show it. Chris had never been afraid to do what she felt she should. The pilot stared at her doubtfully and finally turned back to his controls, still muttering.

The shuttle lifted sluggishly, but there was no great difficulty. Doc could see that there was even some fuel remaining when they slipped into the tube at the orbital station. Chris went out, and other guards came in to free him.

"So long, Dr. Feldman," the pilot called softly as they led him out. Then the guards shoved him through the airlock into the station. Fifteen minutes later he was locked into one of the cabins of the *Iroquois*, with all his possessions stacked beside him.

He grinned wryly. As an honest worker on the *Navaho* he'd been treated like an animal. Now, as a human fiend, he was installed in a luxury cabin of the finest ship of the fleet, with constant spin to give a feeling of weight and more room than the entire tube crew had known.

He roamed the cabin until he found a little collapsible table. He set the electron microscope up on that and plugged it in. It seemed a shame that good equipment should be wasted along with his life. He wondered if they would really throw it out into space with him. Probably they would.

He pushed a button on the call board over the table and asked for the steward. There was a long wait, as if the procedure were being checked with some authority, but finally he received a surly acknowledgement. "Steward. Whatcha want?"

"How's the chance of getting some food?"

"You're on first-class."

They could afford it, Doc decided. He wouldn't cost them much, considering the distance he was going. "Bring me two complete dinners—one Earth-normal and one Mars-normal."

"Okay, Feldman. But if you think you can suicide that way, you're wrong. You may be sick, but you'll be alive when they dump you."

A sharp click interrupted him. "That's enough, Steward. Captain Everts speaking. Dr. Feldman, you have my apologies. Until you reach your destination, you are my passenger and entitled to every consideration of any other passenger except freedom of movement through the ship. I am always available for legitimate complaints."

Feldman shook his head. He'd heard of such men. But he'd thought the species extinct.

The steward brought his food in a thoroughly chastened manner. He managed to find space for it and came to attention. "Is that all—sir?"

For a moment, as the smell of real steak reached him, Doc regretted the fact that his metabolism had been switched. Then he shrugged. A little wouldn't hurt him, though there was no proper nourishment in it. He squeezed some of the gravy and bits of meat into one of his bottles, sticking to his purpose; then he fell to on the rest. But after a few bites, it was queerly unsatisfactory. The seemingly unappealing Mars-normal ragout suited his current tastes better, after all.

Once the steward had cleared away the dishes, Doc went to work. It was better than wasting his time in dread. He might even be able to leave some notes behind.

A gong sounded, and a red light warned him that acceleration was due. He finished with his bottles, put them into the incubator, and piled into his bunk, swallowing one of the tablets of morphetal the ship furnished.

Acceleration had ended, and a simple breakfast was waiting when he awoke. There was also a red flashing light over the call board. He flipped the switch while reaching for the coffee.

"Captain Everts," the speaker said. "May I join you in your cabin?"

"Come ahead," Feldman invited. He cut off the switch and glanced at the clock on the wall. There were less than eleven hours left to him.

Everts was a trim man of forty, erect but not rigid. There was neither friendliness nor hostility in his glance. His words were courteous as Doc motioned toward the tray of breakfast. "I've already eaten, thank you."

He accepted a chair. His voice was apologetic when he began. "This is a personal matter which I perhaps have no right to bring up. But my wife is greatly worried about this plague. I violate no confidence in telling you there is considerable unease, even on Earth, according to messages I have received. The ship physician believes Mrs. Everts may have the plague, but isn't sure of the symptoms. I understand you are quite expert."

Doc wondered about the physician. Apparently there was another man who placed his patients above anything else, though he was probably meticulous about obeying all actual rules. There was no law against listening to a pariah, at least.

"When did she have Selznik's migraine?" he asked.

"About thirteen years ago. We went through it together, shortly after having our metabolism switched during the food shortage of '88."

Doc felt carefully at the base of the Captain's skull; the swelling was there. He asked a few questions, but there could be no doubt.

"Both of you must have it, Captain, though it won't mature for another year. I'm sorry."

"There's no hope, then?"

Doc studied the man. But Everts wasn't the sort to dicker even for his life. "Nothing that I've found, Captain. I have a clue, but I'm still working on it. Perhaps if I could leave a few notes for your physician—"

It was Everts' turn to shake his head. "I'm sorry, Dr. Feldman. I have orders to burn out your cabin when you leave. But thank you." He got to his feet and left as quietly and erectly as he had entered.

Doc tore up his notes bitterly. He paced his cabin slowly, reading out the hours while his eyes lingered on the little bottle of cultures. At times the fear grew in him, but he mastered it. There was half an hour left when he began opening the little bottles and making his films.

He was still not finished when steps echoed down the hall, but he was reasonably sure of his results. The bug could not grow in Earth-normal tissue.

Three men entered the room. One of them, dressed in a spacesuit, held out another suit to him. The other two began gathering up everything in the cabin and stowing it neatly into a sack designed to protect freight for a limited time in a vacuum.

Doc forced his hands to steadiness with foolish pride and began climbing into the suit. He reached for the helmet, but the man shook his head, pointing to the oxygen gauge.

There would be exactly one hour's supply of oxygen when he was thrown out and it still lacked five minutes of the deadline.

They marched him down the hallway, to meet Everts coming toward them. There were still three minutes left when they reached the airlock, with its inner door already open. The spacesuited man climbed into it and began strapping down so that the rush of air would not sweep him outward when the other seal was released.

Doc had saved one bracky weed. Now he raised it to his lips, fumbling for a light.

Everts stepped forward and flipped a lighter. Doc inhaled deeply. Fear was thick in every muscle, and he needed the smoke desperately. Then he caught himself.

"Better change your metabolism back to Earth-normal, Captain Everts," he said, and his voice was so normal that he hardly recognized it.

Everts' eyes widened briefly. The man bowed faintly. "Thank you, Dr. Feldman."

It was ridiculous, impossible, and yet there was a curious relief at the formality of it. It was like something from a play, too unreal to affect his life.

Everts nodded to the man holding the helmet. Doc dropped his bracky weed and felt the helmet snap down. A hiss of oxygen reached him and the suit ballooned out. There was no gravity; the two men handed him up easily to the one in the airlock while the inner seal began to close.

There was still ten seconds to go, according to the big chronometer that had been installed in the lock. The spaceman used it in tying the sack of possessions firmly to Doc's suit.

A red light went on. The man caught Doc and held him against the outer seal. The red light blinked. Four seconds . . . three . . . two. . . .

There was a sudden heavy thudding sound, and the *Iroquois* seemed to jerk sideways slightly. The spaceman's face swung around in surprise.

The red light blinked and stayed on. Zero!

The outer seal snapped open and the spaceman heaved. Air exploded outwards, and Doc went with it. He was alone in space, gliding away from the ship, with oxygen hissing softly through the valve and ticking away his life.

XI

CONVERT

Feldman fought for control of himself, forced himself to think, to hold onto his sanity. It was sheer stupidity, since nothing could have been more merciful than to lose this reality. But the will to be himself was stronger than logic. And bit by bit, he forced the fear and horror away from him until he could examine his situation.

He was spinning slowly, so that stars ahead of him seemed to crawl across his view. The ship was retreating from him already hundreds of yards away. Mars was a shrunken pill far away.

Then something blinked to one side. He turned his head to stare.

A little ship was less than three hundred yards away. He recognized it as a life raft. Now his spin brought him around to face it, and he saw it was parallelling his course. The ejection of the life raft must have caused the thump he'd heard before he was cast adrift.

It meant someone was trying to save him. It meant *life*!

He flailed his arms and beat his legs together, senselessly trying to force himself closer, while trying to guess who could have taken the chance. No one he could think of could have booked passage on the *Iroquois*. There wasn't that much free money in the villages.

Something flashed a hot blue, and the little ship leaped

forward. Whoever was handling it knew nothing about piloting. It picked up too much speed at too great an angle.

Again blue spurts came, but this time matters were even worse. Then there was a long wait before a third try was made. He estimated the course. It would miss him by a good hundred feet, but it was probably the best the amateur pilot could do. The ship drifted closer, but to one side. It would soon pass him completely.

A spacesuited figure suddenly appeared in the tiny airlock, holding a coil of rope. The rope shot out, well thrown. But it was too short. It would pass within ten feet—and might as well have been ten miles for all the good it would do him.

Every film he had seen on space seemed to form a mad jumble in his mind, but he seized on the first idea he could remember. He inhaled deeply and yanked the oxygen tank free. An automatic seal on the suit cut off the connection. He aimed the hissing bottle, fumbling for the manual valve.

It almost worked. It kicked him toward the rope slightly, but most of the energy was wasted in setting him into a wilder spin. He blinked, trying to spot the rope. It was within five feet now.

Again he waited, until he seemed to be in position. This time he threw the bottle away from it. It added spin to his vertical axis, but the rope came into view within arm's reach.

He grasped it, just as his lungs seemed about to burst. He couldn't hold on long enough to tie the rope. . . .

His lungs gave up suddenly, collapsing and then sucking in greedily. Clean air rushed in, letting his head clear. He'd forgotten that the inflated suit held enough oxygen for several minutes.

His body struck the edge of the airlock and a hand

jerked him inside. The outer seal was slammed shut and locked, and there was a hiss of air entering.

He threw back his helmet just as Chris Ryan jerked hers off.

Her voice shook almost hysterically. "Thank God. Dan, I almost gave up!"

"I liked the air out there better," he told her bitterly. "If you'll open the lock again, I'll leave. Or am I supposed to believe this is rescue and that you came along just to save me?"

"I came along to see you killed, as you know very well. Saving you wasn't in my orders."

He grunted and reached for the handle that would release the outer lock. "Better get back inside if you don't want to blow out with me."

"It's up to you, Dan," she told him, and there was all the sincerity in the world in her blue eyes. "I'm on your side now."

He began counting on his fingers. "Let's see. The spare battery, the delay in arresting me, the choice of Matthews—"

"It was all true." Anger began to grow in her eyes. "Dan Feldman, you get inside this raft! If you don't care about me, you might consider the people dying of the plague who need you!"

She'd played her trump, and it took the round. He followed her.

"All right," he said grudgingly. "Spill your story."

She held out a copy of a space radiogram, addressed to Mrs. D. E. Everts, and signed by one of the best doctors on the Lobby Board of Directors.

Regret confirm diagnosis. Topsecret. Repeat topsecret. Martian fever incubates fourteen years, believed highly fatal. No cure, research beginning immediately. Penalty violation topsecret, death all concerned.

"Mrs. Everts rates a topsecret break?" Doc commented dryly. "Come off it, Chris!"

"She's the daughter of Elmers of Space Lobby!" Chris answered. She pointed to the message, underlining words with her finger. "*Fourteen years.* You couldn't have caused it. *Highly fatal.* And people are being told it's only a skin disease. *Research beginning.* But you've already done most of the research. I can see that now. I can see a lot of things."

"You've got me beat then," he said. "I can't see how such a reformed young noblewoman calmly walked over and stole a life raft. I can't see how your brilliant mind concocted this whole scheme in almost no time. And to be honest, I can't even see why Medical Lobby decided to save me at the last minute and sent you to do the job. You didn't have to spy out knowledge from me. I've been trying all along to get it to your Research division."

She sighed and dropped onto a little seat.

"I can't prove my motives. You'll just have to believe me. But it wasn't hard to do what I've done. That shuttle pilot was found in a routine check, stowed away on the life raft. I was with Captain Everts when he was found, so I discovered how to get into the raft. And I heard his whole confession. He wasn't the real pilot. He'd come from the villages to save you. The whole scheme was his. I just used it, hoping I could reach you."

As always her story had a convincing element she shouldn't have known. The pilot's farewell, addressing him as Dr. Feldman, had been too low for her to hear, but it was something that fitted her story. It was probably a deliberate clue to give him hope, to assure him the villages were still trying. It shook his confidence.

"And your motive—your real motive?" he insisted.

She swore at him, then began ripping off the spacesuit. She turned her back, pulling a thin blouse down from her neck. He stared, then reached out to touch the lump there.

"So you've had Selznik's migraine and know you're carrying plague. And you've decided your precious Lobby won't save you?"

She dropped her eyes, then raised them to meet his defiantly. "I'm not just scared and selfish. Dad caught it, too, and it must be close to the time for him. He switched to Mars-normal when he was a liaison agent and never changed back. Dan, are we all going to have to die? Can't you save him?"

Feldman was out of his suit and at the control panel. There was a manual lever, which Chris must have used before. It might work out here where there was room to maneuver and nothing to hit. But trying to make a landing was going to be different.

"Dan?" she repeated.

He shrugged. "I don't know. They've started research too late and they'll be under so much pressure that the real brains won't have a chance. The topsecret stuff looks bad for research. Maybe there's a cure. It works in culture bottles, but it may fail in person. When I'm convinced I'm safe with you, I may tell you about it."

"Oh." Her voice was low. Then she sighed. "I suppose I can understand why you hate me, Dan."

"I don't hate you. I'm too mixed up. Tomorrow maybe, but not now. Shut up and let me see if I can figure out how to land this thing."

He found that the fuel tanks were nearly full, but that still didn't leave much margin. Mars must have been notified by Everts and be ready to pick the raft up. He had to reach the wastelands away from any of the shuttle ports. They had no aspirators, however, and they couldn't cover much territory in the spacesuits they would have to use. It meant he'd have to land close to a village where he was known.

He jockeyed the ship around by trial and error, studying the manual that was lying prominently on the control panel. According to the booklet, the ship was simple to operate. It was self-leveling in an atmosphere, and automatic flare computers were supposed to make it possible for an amateur to judge the rate of descent near the surface. It looked reassuring—and was probably written with that in mind.

Finally he reached for the control, hoping he'd figured his landing orbit reasonably well by simple logic. He smoothed it out in the following hours as he watched the markings on Mars. When they were near turnover point, he began cranking the little gyroscope to swing the ship. It saved fuel to turn without power, and he wasn't sure he could have turned accurately by blasting.

He was gaining some proficiency, however, he felt. But now he had to waste fuel and ruin his orbit again. There was no way to practice maneuvering without actually doing so.

In the end, he compromised, leaving a small margin for a bad landing that would require a second attempt, but with less practice than he wanted.

He had located Jake's village through the little telescope when he finally reached for the main blast control. The thin haze of Mars' atmosphere came rushing up, while the blast lashed out. Then they were in the outer fringes of the sky and the blast was beginning to show a corona that ruined visibility.

He turned to the flare computer and back to what he could see through the quartz viewport. He was going to land about half a mile from the village, as nearly as he could judge.

The computer seemed to work as it should. The speed was within acceptable limits. He gave up trying to see the ground and was forced to trust the machinery designed for amateur pilots. The flare bloomed, and he yanked down on the little lever.

It could have been worse. They hit the ground, bounced twice, and turned over. The ship was a mess when Feldman freed himself from the elastic straps of the seat. Chris had shrieked as they hit, but she was unbuckling herself now.

He threw her her spacesuit and one of the emergency bottles of oxygen from the rack. "Hurry up with that. We've sprung a leak and the pressure's dropping."

They were halfway to the village when a dozen tractors came racing up and Jake piled out of the lead one to drag the two in with him.

"Heard about it from the broadcasts and figured you might land around here. Good to see you, Doc." He started the tractor off at full speed, back to the wastelands, while Doc stared at the armed men who were riding the tractors.

Jake caught his look and nodded. "You're in enemy territory, Doc. There's a war going on!"

XII
WAR

Sometimes it seemed to Doc that war was nothing but an endurance race to see how many times they could run before they were bombed. He was just beginning to drop off to sleep after a long trip for the sixth consecutive day when the little alarm shrilled. He sighed and shook Chris awake.

"Again?" she protested. But she got up and began helping him pack.

Jake came in, his eyes weary, pulling on the old jacket with the big star on its sleeve. Doc hadn't been too surprised to learn that Jake was the actual leader of the rebels. "Shuttles spotted taking off this way. And I still can't find where the leak is. They haven't missed our location once this week. Here, give me that."

He took the electron mike that had been among Doc's' possessions, but Chris recaptured it. "I can manage," she told him, and headed out for the tractor where Lou was waiting.

Doc scowled after her. He and Jake had been watching her. She was too useful to Doc's research to be turned away, but they didn't trust her yet. So far, however, they had found nothing wrong with her conduct. Still. . . .

He swung suddenly into Jake's tractor. "Just remembered something. How'd they find me that time I stopped in the tractor to use the mike? I was pretty well hidden, and no tracks last in the sand long enough for them to have followed. But they were there when I came to. Somehow, they must have put a radio tracer on me."

Jake waited while they lighted up, his eyes suddenly bright. "You mean something you got from her house was bugged? It figures."

"And I've still got all the stuff. Now they find wherever we set up headquarters, though they've always managed to miss my laboratory, even when they've hit the troops around us. Jake, I think it's the microscope." Doc managed to push enough junk off one of the seats to make a cramped bed, and stretched out. "Sure, we figured they sent her because they want to keep tabs on what I discover. They've finally gotten scared of the plague, and she's the perfect Judas goat. But they have to have some way to get in touch with her. I'll bet there's a tracer in the mike and a switch so she can modulate it or key it to send out Morse."

"Yeah," Jake nodded. "Well, she does her own dirty work. I might get to like her if she was on our side. Okay, Doc. If they've put things into the mike, I've got a boy who'll find and fix it so she won't guess it's been touched."

Doc relaxed. For the moment, there would be no power in the instrument, nor any excuse for her to use it. But she must have handled some secret arrangement during the work periods. She used the mike more than he did. The switch could be camouflaged easily enough. If anyone detected the signal, they'd probably only think it was some leak in the electrical circuit.

Far away, the shuttle rockets had appeared as tiny dots in the sky. They were standing on their tails a second later, just off the ground, letting the full force of their blasts bake the area where headquarters had been.

Jake watched grimly, driving by something close to instinct. Then he looked back. "Know anything about a Dr. Harkness?"

"Not much, except that he protested sealing off the villages. Why?"

"He and five other doctors were picked up, trying to get through to us. Claimed they wanted to give us medical help. We can use them, God knows. I guess I'll have to chance it."

They stopped at a halfway village and hid the tractors before looking for a place to rest. Doc found Chris curled up asleep against the microscope. He had a hard time getting her to leave it in the tractor, but she was too genuinely tired to put up any real argument.

Jake reported in the morning before they set out again. "You were right, Doc. It was a nice job of work. Must have taken the best guys in Southport to hide the circuit so well. But it's safe now. It just makes a kind of meaningless static nobody can trace. Maybe we can get you a permanent lab now."

Doc debated again having Chris left behind and decided against it. The Lobby was determined to let him find a cure for them if he could. That meant Chris would work herself to exhaustion trying to help. Let her think she was doing it for the Lobby! It was time she was on the receiving end of a double cross.

"It's a stinking way to run a war," he decided.

Jake chuckled without much humor. "It's the war you wanted, remember? They forced our hand, but it had to come sometime. Right now the Lobby's fighting to get their hands on your work before we can use it; they're just using holding tactics, which helps our side. And we're hoping you get the cure so we can win. With that, maybe we'll whip them."

It was a crazy war, with each side killing more of its own men than of the enemy. The runners were increasing, and

Jake's army was learning to shoot the poor devils mercifully and go on. They knew, at least, that there was no current danger of infection. In the Lobby towns, more were dying of panic in their efforts to escape the runners.

Desert towns had joined the villages, reluctantly but inevitably, to give the rebels nearly three-quarters of the total population. But the Lobby forces and the few cities held most of the real fighting equipment and they were ready to wait until Earth could send out unmanned rockets, loaded with atomics, which could cut through space at ten times normal speed.

There were vague lines of battle, but time was the vital factor. The Lobbies waited to steal a cure for the plague and the villages waited until they could announce it and demand surrender as its price.

It looked as if both sides were doomed to disappointment, however. He and Chris had put in every spare minute between moving and the minimum of sleep in searching for something that would check the disease. It couldn't grow in an Earth-normal body, but it didn't die, either. And there wasn't enough normal food available to permit the switchover for more than a handful of people. Even Earth was out of luck, since eighty percent of her population ate synthetics. There were ways to synthesize Earth-normal food, but they were still hopelessly inefficient.

Jake had ordered one of the villages to rebuild their plant for such a purpose, while another was producing the enzyme that would permit switching. But it looked hopeless for more than a few of the most valuable men.

"No progress?" Jake asked for the hundredth time.

Doc grinned wryly. "A lot, but no help. We've found a fine accelerator for the bug. We can speed up its incubation or even make someone already infected catch it all over again. But we can't slow it down or stop it."

The new laboratory was still being fitted when they arrived. It had been dug into one of the few real cliffs in this section of Mars. The power plant had been installed, complete with a steam plant that would operate off sunlight in the daytime through a series of heat valves that took in a lot of warm air and produced smaller amounts hot enough to boil water.

"I'll see you whenever I can," Jake said. "But mostly, you're going to be somewhat isolated so they won't trace you. Let them think they goofed with the shuttles and hit you and Chris. Anything you need?"

"Guinea pigs," Doc told him sarcastically. It was meant as a joke, though a highly bitter one. Jake nodded and left them.

Doc opened the cots as Chris came in, not bothering to unpack the equipment. "Hit the sack, Chris," he told her.

She looked at him doubtfully. "You almost said that the way you'd address a human being, Dan. You're slipping. One of these days you'll like me again."

"Maybe." He was too tired to argue. "I doubt it, though. Forget it and get some sleep."

She watched him silently until he got up to turn out the light. Then she sighed heavily. "Dan?"

"Yeah?"

"I never got a divorce. The publicity would have been bad. But anyway, we're still married."

"That's nice." He swung to face her briefly. "And they found the radio in the microscope. Better get to sleep, Chris."

"Oh." It was a quiet exclamation, barely audible. There was a sound that might have been a sniffle if it had come from anyone else. Then she rolled over. "All right, Dan. I still want to help you."

He cursed himself for a stupid fool for telling her.

Fatigue was ruining what judgment he had. From now on, he'd have to watch her every minute. Or had she really seen the value of the research by now? She wasn't a fool. It should have registered on even her stubborn mind. But he was too sleepy to think about it.

She had breakfast ready in the morning. She made no comment on what had been said during the night. Instead, she began discussing a way to keep one of the organic anti-biotics from splitting into simpler compounds when they tried to switch it over to Mars-normal. They were both hopelessly bad chemists and biologists, but there was no one else to do the work.

Chris worked harder than ever during the day.

Just after sundown, Jake came in with a heavy box. He dropped it onto the floor. "Mice!"

Doc ripped off the cover, exposing fine screening. There were at least six dozen mice inside!

"Harkness found them," Jake explained. "A hormone extraction plant used them for testing some of the products. Had them sent by regular shipments from Earth. Getting them cost a couple of men, but Harkness claims it's worth it. He's a good man on a raid. Here!"

He'd gone to the doorway again and came back with another box, this one crammed with bottles and boxes. "They had quite a laboratory, and Harkness picked out whatever he thought you could use."

Chris and Doc were going through it. The labels were engineering ones, but the chemical formulae were identification enough. There were dozens of chemicals they hadn't hoped to get.

"Anything else?" Doc finally asked as they began arranging the supplies.

"More runners. A lot more. We're still holding things down, but it's reaching a limit. Panic will start in the camps if this keeps on. But that's my worry. You stick to yours."

Several of the new chemicals showed promise in the tubes. But two of them proved fatal to the mice and the others were completely innocuous in the little animal's bodies, both to mouse and to germ. The plague was much hardier in contact with living cells than in the artificial environment of the culture jars.

They lost seven mice in two days, but that seemed unimportant; the females were already living up to their reputations, nearly all pregnant. Doc didn't know the gestation period, but he remembered that it was short.

"Funny they all started at the same time," he commented. "Must have been shipped out separately or else been kept apart while they were switched over to Mars-normal. Something interrupted their habits, anyhow."

A few nights later they learned what it was. There was a horrible squealing that woke him out of the depths of his sleep. Chris was already at the light switch. As light came on, they turned to the mouse box.

All the animals were charging about in their limited space, their little legs driving madly and their mouths open. What they lacked in size they made up in numbers, and the din was terrific.

But it didn't last. One by one, the mice began dropping to the floor of the cage. In fifteen minutes, they were all dead!

It was obviously the plague, contracted after having their metabolism switched. Women were sterile for some time after Selznik's migraine struck, and the same must have been true of the mice. They must have contracted the plague at about the same time and reached fertility together. Somehow, the plague incubation period had been shortened to fit their life span; the disease was nothing if not adaptive.

Chris prepared a slide in dull silence. The familiar cell was there when Doc looked through the microscope. He picked up one of the little creatures and cut it open, removing one of the foetuses.

"Make a film of that," he suggested.

She worked rapidly, scraping out the almost microscopic brain, dissolving out the fatty substance, and transferring the result to a film. This time, even at full magnification, there was no sign of the filaments that were always present in diseased flesh. The results were the same for the other samples they made.

"Something about the very young animal or a secretion from the mother's organs keeps the bug from working." Doc reached for a bracky weed and accepted a light from Chris without thinking of it. "Every kid I've heard about contracted the plague between the second and third year. None are born with it, none get it earlier. I've suspected this, but now here's confirmation."

Chris began preparing specimens, while Doc got busy with tubes of the culture. They'd have to test various fluids from the tiny bodies, but there were enough cultures prepared. Then, if the substance only inhibited growth, there would be a long, slow test; if it killed the bugs, they might know more quickly.

Jake came in before the final tests, but waited on them. Doc was studying a film in the microscope. He suddenly motioned excitedly for Chris.

"See the filaments? They're completely disintegrated. And there's one of the big cells broken open. We've got it! It's in the blood of the foetus. And it must be in the blood of newborn children, too!"

Jake looked at the slide, but his face was doubtful.

"Maybe you've got something, Doc. I hope so. And I hope you can use it." He shook his head wearily. "We need good news right now. A couple of big rockets just reached the station and they've been sending shuttles back and forth a mile a minute. Nobody can figure how they got here so fast or what they're for. But it doesn't look good for us!"

XIII

SUSCEPTIBILITY

Doc could feel the tension in the village where GHQ was temporarily located long before they were close enough for details to register. The people were gathered in clusters, staring at the sky where the station must be. A few were pacing up and down, gesticulating with tight sweeps of their arms.

One woman suddenly went into even more violent action. She leaped into the air and then took off at a rapid trot, then a run. Her hands were tearing at her clothes and her mouth seemed to be working violently. She was halfway to the top of the nearest dune before a rifle cracked. She dropped, to twitch once and lie still.

Almost with her death, another figure leaped from one of the houses, his face bare of the necessary aspirator. He took off at a violent run, but he was falling from lack of air before the bullet ended his struggles.

The people suddenly began to move apart, as if trying to get away from each other. For weeks they had faced the horror with courage; now it was finally too much for them.

Tension mounted as no news came from the cities. Doc noticed that it seemed to aggravate or speed up the disease. He saw three men shot in the next half hour.

He was trying to calm them with word of a possible cure for the plague, but their reactions were as curiously dull as those of Jake had been. As he spoke, they faced him with set expressions. At his mention of the need for the blood of young children, they turned from him, sullenly silent.

Jake came over, nodding unhappily. "It's what I was afraid might happen, Doc. George Lynn! Tell Doc what's wrong."

Lynn was reluctant, but he finally stumbled out his explanation. "It ain't like you, Doc. Comes from that Lobby woman you got. It's her dirty idea. We've seen the Lobby doctors cutting open our kids, poisoning their blood, and bleeding them dry. That ain't gonna happen again, Doc. You tell her it ain't!"

Doc swore as he realized their ignorance. An unexplained vaccination looked like poisoning of the blood. But he couldn't understand the bleeding part until Jake filled him in.

"Northport infant's wing. Each department has its own blood bank and donation is compulsory. Southport started it a couple months ago, too."

The long arm of the Lobby had reached out again. Now if he ever got them to try the treatment, it would be only after long sessions of preparing them with the facts, and there was hardly enough time for the crucial work!

By afternoon, Judge Ben Wilson reached them. His voice shook with fatigue as he climbed up to address the crowd through a power megaphone. "Southport's going crazy." He had to pause for breath between each sentence. "Earth's pulling back all the important people. They're packing them into the ships. They're leaving only colonials with no Earth rights. Those ships left when they decided the plague was coming from here. They won't let anybody back until the plague is licked. There won't be an Earth technician on Mars tomorrow."

"No bombs?" someone called.

"No bombs. The ships must have started before you rebelled, maybe meant honestly to save their own kind. But now it's a military action, and don't think it won't mean trouble. The poor devils in the city bet on the wrong horse. Now they can't run their food factories or anything else for long. Not without technicians. They've got to whip you now. Up to this time, they've been fighting for the Lobbies. Now they'll fight you for their own bellies to get your supplies. And they've still got shuttle rockets and fuel for them. Now beat it. I gotta confer with Jake."

Doc started after the judge, but Dr. Harkness caught his arm and drew him aside. Chris followed.

"I've found another epidemic," Harkness told them. "Over at Marconi. It's kept me on the run all night, and now half the village is down with it. Starts like a common cold, runs a fair fever, and the skin breaks out all over with bright red dots. . . ."

He went on describing it. Chris began asking him about what medical supplies he had brought with him, pilfered from Northport hospital. She seemed to know what it was, but refused to say until she saw the cases. Doc also preferred to wait. Sometimes things weren't as bad as they seemed, though usually they were worse.

Marconi was dead to all outward appearances, with nobody on the streets. It had been a village of great hopes a week before, since this was where they had decided to experiment with switching the people back to Earth-normal. They'd had the best chance of survival of anyone on Mars until this came up.

Three people lay on the beds in the first house Harkness led them to. The room was darkened, and a man was stumbling around, trying to tend the others, though the little spots showed on his skin. He grinned weakly. "Hi, Doc. I guess we're making a lot of trouble, ain't we?"

Chris gave Doc no chance to answer. "Just as I thought. Measles! Plain old-fashioned measles."

"Figured so," the sick man said. "Like my brother back on Earth."

The others looked doubtful, but Doc reassured them. Chris should know; she'd worked in a swanky hospital where the patients were mostly Earth-normal. Measles was one of the diseases which was foiled by the metabolism switch. Well, at least they wouldn't have to be quarantined here.

Chris finished treating the family with impersonal efficiency, discussing the symptoms loudly with Harkness. "It's a good thing it isn't serious!"

"No," Harkness answered bitterly. "Not serious. It's only killed five children and three adults so far!"

"It would, here," Doc agreed unhappily. He led Chris out of the room on the pretext of washing his hands. "It's serious enough to force us to abandon the whole idea of going back to Earth-normal. Measles today, smallpox, tuberculosis, scarlet fever and everything else tomorrow. These people have lived Mars-normal so long their natural immunity has been destroyed. On Earth where the disease was everywhere, kids used to pick up some immunity with constant exposure, even without what might be called a case of the disease. Here, the blood has no reason to build antibodies. They can be killed by things people used to laugh at. How the disease got here, I don't know. But it's here. So we'll have to give up the idea of switching back to Earth-normal."

He gathered up one of the kits and started toward the other houses. "And Lord knows how long it will take to get the blood for the other treatment, even if it works."

They worked as a team for a while, with Harkness frowning as he watched Chris. Finally the young doctor stopped Chris outside the fifth house. "These are my patients, Dr. Ryan. I left the Lobby because I didn't believe colonials were mere livestock. I still feel the same. I appreciate your help in diagnosis and methods of treatment. But I can't let you handle my patients this way."

"Dan!" She swung around with eyes glazing. "Dan, are you going to stand for that?"

"I think you'd better wait in the tractor, Chris."

He was lucky enough to catch the kit she threw at him before its precious contents spilled. But it wasn't luck that guided his hand to the back of her skirt hard enough to leave it stinging.

Her face froze and she stormed out. A moment later they heard the tractor start off.

But Doc had no time to think of her. He and Harkness split up and began covering the streets, house by house, while he passed on the word to abandon the metabolism switch and go back to Mars-normal.

Jake sent two other doctors to relieve them late in the evening. Things were somewhat quieter at GHQ as Doc reported the events at Marconi.

"Where's Dr. Ryan?" Jake asked at last.

Doc exchanged glances with Harkness. "She isn't in the lab?"

"Wasn't there an hour ago."

Doc cursed himself for letting her go. With the knowledge that the radio in the mike was disabled, she'd obviously grabbed the first chance to report back. And with her had gone news of the only cure they had found.

Jake took it as philosophically as he could, though it was a heavy blow to his hopes. They spent half the night looking for her tractor, on the chance that she might have gotten lost or broken down, but there was no sign of it.

She was waiting in the laboratory when he returned at

dawn. Her face was dirty and her uniform was a mess. But she was smiling. She got up to greet him, holding out two large bottles.

"Infant plasma—straight from Southport. And if you think I had it easy lying my way in and out of the hospital, you're a fool, Dan Feldman. If the man who took my place there hadn't been a native idiot, I never would have gotten away with it."

The things he had suspected could still be right, he realized. She could have reported everything to the Lobby. It was a better explanation than her vague account of bullying her way in and out. But she'd had a rough drive, and he wanted the plasma. Curiously, he was glad to have her back with him. He reached out a hand for the bottles.

She put the bottle on the table and grabbed up a short-bladed knife. "Not so fast," she cried. Her eyes were blazing now. "Dan Feldman, if you touch those bottles until you've crawled across the floor on your face and apologized for the way you treated me the last few days, I'll cut your damned heart out."

He shook his head, chuckling at the picture she made. There were times when he could almost see why he'd married her.

"All right, Chris," he gave in. "I'll be darned if I'll crawl, but you've earned an apology. Okay?"

She sighed uncertainly. Then she nodded and began changing for work.

XIV

IMMUNITY

They worked through the day in what seemed to be armed truce. There was no coffee waiting for him when he awoke next, as he'd come to expect, but he didn't comment. He went to where she was already working, checking on the results of the plasma on the cultures.

The response had been slower than with the mouse blood, but now the bugs seemed to be dead. The filaments were destroyed, and there were no signs of the big cells. It seemed to be a cure, at least in the culture bottles.

"We'll need volunteers," he decided. "There should be animals, but we don't have any. At least this stuff isn't toxic. We need a natural immune and someone infected. Two of each, so one can be treated and the other used for a control. Makes four. Not enough to be sure, but it will have to do."

"Two," Chris corrected. "You're not infected, I am."

"Two others," he agreed. "I'll get them from Jake."

Most of GHQ was out on the street, but Doc found Jake inside the big schoolroom where he enjoyed his early morning bracky and coffee. The chief listened and agreed at once, turning to the others in the room.

"Who's had the jumping headache? Okay, Swanee. Who never had it?" He blinked in surprise as three men nodded out of the eight present. "I guess you go, Tom."

The two men stood up, tamping out their weeds, and went out with Doc.

Chris had everything set up. They matched coins to decide who would be treated. Doc noticed that Chris would get no plasma, while he was scheduled for everything. He watched her prepare the culture and add the accelerator that would speed development and make certain he and Tom were infected, then let her inject it.

That was all, except for the waiting. To keep conditions more closely alike, they were to stay there until the tests were finished, not even eating for fear of upsetting the conditions. Swanee dug out a pack of worn cards and began to deal while Doc dug out some large pills to use as chips.

It was an hour later when the pain began. Doc had just won the pot of fifty pills and opened his mouth for the expected gloating. He yelled as an explosion seemed to go off inside his head. Even closing his mouth was agony.

A moment later, Tom began to sweat. It got worse, spreading to the whole area of the back of the head and neck. Doc lay on the cot, envying Chris and Swanee who had already been infected naturally. He longed desperately for bracky, and had to keep reminding himself that no drugs must upset the tests. It was the longest day he had ever spent, and he began to doubt that he could get through it. He watched the little clock move from one minute to nine over to half a minute and hung breathless until it hit the nine. There was no question about whether the infection had taken. Now they could dull the agony.

Chris had the anodyne tablets already dissolved in water, and Swanee was passing out three lighted bracky weeds. It took a few minutes for the relief of the anodyne, and even that couldn't kill all the pain. But it didn't matter by comparison. He sucked the weed, mashed it out and began dealing the cards again.

They had a plentiful supply of the anodyne and used it liberally during the night. The test was a speeded-up simulation of the natural course of the disease, where painkiller would take time to get for most people here, but would then be used generously.

Precisely at nine in the morning, Chris began to inject Swanee and Doc with plasma.

Now there was no thought of cards. They waited, trying to talk, but with most of their attention on the clock. Doc had estimated that an hour should be enough to show results, but it was hard to remember that an hour was the guess as to the minimum time.

He winced as Chris took a tiny bit of flesh from his neck. She went to the other men, and then submitted to his work on herself. Then she began preparing the slides.

"Feldman," she read the name of the slide as she inserted it into the microscope. Then her breath caught sharply. "Only dead cells!"

It was the same for Swanee and Tom. Each had to look at his own slide and have it explained before the results could be believed. But at last Chris bent over her own slide. A minute later she glanced up, nodding. "What it should be. It checks."

Tom whooped and went out the door to notify Jake. There was only plasma for some two hundred injections, but that should yield sufficient proof. Once salvation was offered, there should be no trouble convincing the people that blood donations from their children were worthwhile.

Later, when the last of the plasma had been used, they could finally relax. Chris slipped off her smock and dropped onto the cot. A tired smile came onto her lips. "You're forgiven, Dan," she said. A moment later she was obviously asleep. Doc meant to join her, but it was too much effort. He leaned his head forward onto his arms, vaguely wondering why she was calling off the feud.

It was night outside when he awoke, and he was lying on the cot, though he still felt cramped and strained. He stirred, groaning, and finally realized that a hand was on his shoulder shaking him. He looked up to see Jake above him. Chris was busy with the coffee maker.

Jake slumped onto the cot beside Doc. "We took Southport," he announced.

That knocked the sleep out of Doc's system. "You what?"

"We took it, lock, stock and barrel. I figured the news of your cure would put guts into the men, and it did. But we'd probably have taken it anyhow. There wasn't anything to fight for there after Earth pulled out and the plague really hit. Wilson mistook last-minute panic for fighting spirit. The poor devils didn't have anything to fight about, once the Lobby stopped goading them."

Doc tried to assimilate the news. But once the surprise was gone, he found it meant very little. Maybe his revolutionary zeal had cooled, once the Lobby men had pulled out. "We'll need a lot more plasma than there is in Southport," he said.

"Not so much, maybe," Jake denied. "Doc, three of the men you injected were shot down as runners. Your plasma's no good."

"It takes time to work, Jake. I told you there might be a case or two that would be too close to the edge. Three is more than I expected; but it's not impossible."

"There was plenty of time. They blew after we got back from Southport." Jack dropped his hand on Doc's shoulder, and his face softened. "Harkness tested every man you injected. He finished half an hour ago. Five showed dead bugs. The rest of them weren't helped at all."

Doc fumbled for a weed, trying to think. But his thoughts refused to focus. "Five!"

"Five out of two hundred. That's about average. And what about Tom? He was jumping around after the test last night, telling how you'd cured him, how he'd seen the dead bugs; but he never had the jumping headache, and you never gave him the plasma! He's got dead bugs, though. Harkness tested him."

Doc let his realization of his own idiocy sink in until he could believe it. Jake was right. Tom had never been treated, yet Chris had reported dead bugs. They'd all been so ready to believe in miracles that no one had been able to think straight after the long wait.

"There was a bump on his neck—a small one," he said slowly. "Jake, he must have caught it, even if he seemed immune. If he was taking anodyne anyway for something— or unconscious—"

"He was up in Northport six years ago for a kidney operation," Jake admitted doubtfully. "We had to chip in to pay for it. But you still didn't treat him, and he's cured. Face it, Doc, that plasma is no good inside the body."

His hand tightened on Doc's shoulder again. "We're not blaming you. We don't judge a man here except by what he is. Maybe the stuff helps a little. We'll go on using it when we get it; tell everybody you were a mite optimistic, so they'll figure it's a gamble, but have a little hope left. And you keep trying. Something cured it in Tom. Now you find out what."

Doc watched him go out numbly, and turned to Chris.

"It can't be right," she said shakily. "You and Swanee were cured. Maybe it was the accelerator. It had to be some- thing."

"You didn't have the accelerator," he accused.

"No, and I've still got live bugs. I was never supposed to be cured, so I expected to see just what I saw. How I missed the fact that Tom should have been like me, I don't know. Damn it, oh, damn it!"

He's never seen her cry before, except in fury. But she mastered it almost at once, shaking tears out of her eyes. "All right. Plasma works in a bottle but not in an adult body. Maybe something works in the body but not in a bottle."

"Maybe. And maybe some people are just naturally immune after it reaches a certain stage. Maybe we ran into coincidence."

But he didn't believe that, any more than she did. The answer had to be in the room. He'd taken a massive dose of the disease and been cured in a few hours.

Outside the room, the war went on, drawing toward a close. The supposed partial cure was good propaganda, if nothing else, and Jake was widening his territory steadily. There was only token resistance against him. He had the Southport shuttles now to cover huge areas in a hurry. But inside the room, the battle was less successful. It wasn't the accelerator. It wasn't the tablets of anodyne. They even tried sweeping the floor and using the dust without results.

Then another test in the room, made with four volunteers Jake selected, yielded complete cures after injections with plain salt water in place of plasma.

The plague speeded up again. About four people out of a hundred now seemed to have caught the disease and cured themselves. They accounted for what faith was left in Doc's plasma and gave some unfounded hope to the others.

Northport fell a week later, putting the whole planet in rebel hands.

Jake returned, wearier than ever. He'd proved to be one of the natural immunes, but the weight of the campaign that could only end in a defeat by the plague left him no room to rejoice in his personal fortune.

This time he looked completely defeated. And a moment later, Doc saw why as Jake flipped a flimsy sheet onto the table. It bore the seals of Space and Medical Lobbies.

Jake pointed upwards. "The war rockets are there, all right. We knew they'd come. Now all they want for calling them off is our surrender and your cure. If they don't get both, they'll blow the planet to bits. We have two days."

The rockets could be seen clearly with binoculars. There were more than enough to destroy all life on the planet. Maybe they'd be used eventually, anyhow, since the Lobbies wanted no more rebellion. But with a cure for the plague, he might have bought them off.

Chris stood beside him, looking as if it were a bitter pill for her, too. She'd risked herself in the hands of the enemy, had cooperated with him in everything she'd been taught to oppose, and had worked like a dog. Now the Lobbies seemed to forget her as a useless tool. They were falling back on a raw power play and forgetting any earlier schemes.

"Maybe they'd hold off for a while if I agreed to go to them and share all my ideas, specimens and notes," he said at last. "Do you think your Lobby would settle for that, Chris?"

"I don't know, Dan. I've stopped thinking their way." She seemed almost apologetic for the admission.

He dropped an arm over her shoulder and turned with her back to the laboratory. "Okay, then we've got to find a miracle. We've got two days ahead of us. At least we can try."

But he knew he was lying to himself. There wasn't anything he could think of to try.

XV
DECISION

Two days was never enough time for a miracle. Doc decided as he packed his notes into a small bag and put it beside his bundle of personal belongings. He glanced around the room for the last time, and managed a grin at Jake's gloomy expression.

"Maybe I can bluff them, or maybe they'll string along for a while," he said. "Anyhow, now that they've agreed to take me and my notes in place of the cure we're fresh out of, I've got to be on that shuttle when it goes back to their men at orbital station."

Jake nodded. "I don't like selling friends down the river, Doc. But it wouldn't do you any more good to blow up with the planet, I reckon. They won't call off the war rockets when they do get you, of course. But maybe they won't use them, except as a threat to put the Lobbies back in, stronger than ever."

He stuck out one of his awkwardly shaped hands, clapped the aspirator over his face and hurried out. Doc picked up his bags and went toward the little tractor where Lou was waiting to drive him and Chris back toward Southport and the shuttle rocket that would be landing for them. They hadn't mentioned Chris in their demands, but her father must expect her to return.

After they had him, he'd be on his own. His best course

was probably to insist on talking only to Ryan at Medical Lobby, and then being completely honest. The room here would be kept sealed, in case the Lobby wanted to investigate where he had failed. And his notes were honest, which was something that could usually be determined. Chris could testify to that, anyhow, since she'd kept a lot of them for him.

At best, there would be a chance for some compromise and perhaps some clue for them that might eventually end the plague. They had enough men to work on it, and billions in equipment. At worst, he should gain a little time.

"Cheer up, Chris," he told her as he climbed through the little airlock. "Maybe Harkness will turn up the cure before our negotiations break down. He has the whole of Northport Hospital to play with. They haven't tried to chase him out of there yet. After all, we almost found something with no equipment except wild imaginations."

She shook her head as the tractor began moving. "Shut up! I've got enough trouble without your coming down with logorrhea. Don't be a fool."

"Why change now?" he asked her. "Everything I've done has been because I am a fool. I guess my luck lasted longer than I could expect. And I'm still fool enough to think that the solution has to turn up eventually. We know it has to be in that room. Damn it, we must know it—if we could only think straight now."

She reached over and touched his hand, but made no comment. They had been over that statement of desperation too many times already. But it kept nagging at him— something in the room, something in the room! Something so common that nobody noticed it!

They passed a crowd chasing down a runner. Something in that room could have saved the unlucky man. It could have saved Mars, perhaps.

He growled for the hundredth time, cursing his fatigue-numbed mind. Too little sleep, too much coffee and bracky. . . .

He reached for the package of weed, realizing that he would miss it on Earth, if he ever got there. Like everything here on the planet, he'd begun by detesting it and wound up finding it the thing he wanted to keep forever. He lighted the bracky and sat smoking, watching Lou drive. When the first was finished, he lighted another from the butt.

She put out a hand and took it away. "Please, Dan. I can stand the stuff, but I'll never like it, and the tractor's stuffy enough already. I've taken enough of it. And it keeps reminding me of our test—the three of you stinking up the place, puffing and blowing that out, while I couldn't even get a breath of air. . . ."

She was getting logorrhea herself now and—

The answer finally hit him! He jerked around, making a grab for Lou's shoulder, motioning for the man to head back.

"Bracky—it has to be! Chris, that's it. Jake picked out the second group of men from his friends—and they are all cronies because they hang around so much in their so-called smoking room. The first time, it killed the bugs for all of us who smoked—and it didn't work for you because you never learned the habit."

Lou had the tractor turned and the rheostat all the way to the floor.

She was sitting up now, but she wasn't fully satisfied. "The percentage of immunes seems about right. But why do some of the smokers get the disease while some don't?"

"Why not? It depends on whether they pick up the habit before or after the disease gets started. Tom must have got his while he was in Northport. They wouldn't let him smoke there—if he had the habit before, for that matter."

She found no fault with that. He twisted it back and forth in his mind, trying to find a fault. There seemed to be none. The only trouble was that they couldn't send a message that bracky was the cure and hope that Earth would prove it true. No polite note of apology would do after that. They had to be sure. Too many other ideas had proved wrong already.

Jake saw them coming and came running toward the laboratory, but Lou stopped the tractor before it reached the building and let the older man in.

"Get me a dozen men who have the plague. I want the worst cases you have, and ones that Harkness tested himself," Doc ordered. "And then start praying that the cure we've got works fast."

Chris was at the electron mike at once, but one of her hands reached out for the weed. She began puffing valiantly, making sick faces. Now other men began coming in, their faces struggling to find hope, but not daring to believe yet. Jake followed them.

"We'll test at ten-minute intervals. That will be about two hours for the last from the group," Doc decided. One of the doctors Harkness had brought to the villages was busy cutting tiny sections from the lumps on the men's necks, while Chris ran them through the microscope to make sure the bugs were still alive. The regular optical mike was strong enough for that.

Doc handed each man a bracky weed, with instructions to keep smoking, no matter how sick it made him.

There were no results at the end of ten minutes when the first test was made. The second, at the end of twenty minutes, was still infected with live bugs. At the half hour, Chris frowned.

"I can't be sure—take a look, Dan."

He bent over, moving the slide to examine another spot.

"I think so. The next one should tell."

There was no doubt about the fourth test. The bugs were dead, without a single exception that they could find.

One by one, the men were tested and went storming out, shouting the news. For a minute, the gathering crowd was skeptical, remembering the other failures. Then, abruptly, men were screaming, crying and fighting for the precious bracky, like the legions of the damned grabbing for lottery tickets when the prize was a passport to paradise.

Jake swore as he moved toward the door. "We're low on bracky here. Have to get a supply from Edison, I guess, and cart it to the shuttle. Enough for a sample, and to make them want more. It'll be tough, but we'll get it there in time—by the time the shuttle should be picking you up. Doc, you've won our war! From now on, if Earth wants to keep her population up, we'll be a free planet!"

Chris turned slowly from the microscope, holding a slide in her hands. "My bugs," she said unbelievingly. "Dan, they're dead!"

Jake patted her shoulder. "That makes it perfect, girl. Now come on. We've got to start celebrating a victory!"

It was the general feeling of most of the heads of the villages when they met the next day in Southport, using the courtroom that had been presided over so long by Judge Ben Wilson. It was victory, and to the victor belonged the spoils. The bracky had gone out to Earth on a converted war rocket that could make the trip in less than two weeks, and one packet had been specially labeled for Captain Everts. But Earth had already confirmed the cure. The small amounts of the herb found in the botanical collections had been enough to satisfy all doubts.

Harkness, Chris and Doc had been fighting against the desire to rob Earth blind that filled most of the men here for hours now. Now they had the backing of Jake and Ben Wilson. And now finally they leaned back, sensing that the argument had been won.

Bargaining was all right in its place, but it had no place in affairs of life and death such as this. They had to see that Earth received all the bracky she needed. It was only right to charge a fair price for it, but they couldn't restrict it by withholding or overcharging. And they could still gain their ends without blackmail.

Martian alkaloids were tricky things, and bracky smoke contained a number of them. It would take Earth at least ten years to discover and synthesize the right one—and it would still probably cost more than it would to import the weed from Mars. As long as the source of that weed was here, and in the hands of the colonials, there would be no danger of Earth's bombing the planet.

Harkness got up to underscore a point Wilson had made. "The plague lived a million years, and it won't disappear now. The jumping headache, or Selznick's migraine, is unpleasant enough to make us reasonably sure that there will be a steady consumption of the weed. Our problem will be to keep the children from using too much of it, probably." He pulled a weed out and lighted it, puckering his face as the smoke bit his tongue. "I'm told that this gets to be an enjoyable habit. If I can believe that, surely you can believe me when I say we don't have to bargain with lives."

The village men were human, and most of them could remember the strain they had been under when they expected those they loved to die at any hour. It had made them crave vengeance, but now as they had a chance to reexamine it, they began to find it harder to impose the horror of any such threat on others. The final vote was almost unanimous.

Doc listened as they wrangled over the wording of the message to Earth, feeling disconnected from it. He passed

Chris a bracky and lighted it for her. She took it automatically, smiling as the smoke hit her lungs. It was one thing they had in common now, at least.

Ben Wilson finally read the message.

"To the people of Earth, greetings!

"On behalf of the free people of Mars, I have the honor to announce that this planet hereby declares itself a sovereign and independent world. We shall continue to regard Earth as our mother, and to consider the health and welfare of her people in no way second to our own in matters which affect both planets. We trust that Earth will share this feeling of mutual friendship. We trust that all strains of hostility will be ended. The advantages to each from peaceful commerce make any course other than the most cordial of relations unthinkable.

"We shall consider proof of such friendship an order by Earth to all rockets circling this planet that they shall deliver themselves safely into our hands, in order that we may begin converting them to peaceful purposes for the trade that is to come. In turn, we pledge that all efforts will be made to ensure a prompt delivery of those products most in demand, including the curative bracky plant."

He turned to Doc then. "You want to sign it, Dr. Feldman? Make it as acting president or something, until we can get around to voting you into permanent office."

"You and Jake fight over the job," Doc told him. "No, Ben, I mean it."

He got up and moved out into the outer room, where he could avoid the stares of amazement that were turned to him. He'd never asked for the honor, and he didn't want it.

Chris came with him. Her face was shocked and something was slowly draining out of it as he looked at her.

"Forget it, Chris," he said. "You're going back to Earth. There is nothing for you here."

She hadn't quite given up. "There could be, Dan. You know that."

"No. No, Chris, I don't think there ever can be. You can't find a man strong enough to rule who'll be weak enough to let you rule in his place. It didn't work on Earth, and it won't work here. Forget the dreams you had of what could be done with a new planet. Those are the dreams that made a mess of the old one."

"I'll be back," she told him. "Some day I'll be back."

He shook his head again. "No. You wouldn't like what you find here. Freedom is heady stuff, but you have to have a taste for it. You can't acquire a fondness for it secondhand. And for a while, there's going to be freedom here. Besides, once you get back to Earth, you'll forget what happened here."

She sighed at last. For the first time since he had known her, she seemed to give in completely. And for that brief moment, he loved what she could have been, but never would be.

"All right, Dan," she said quietly. "I can't fight you. I never could, I see now. I'll take the rocket back. What are you going to do?"

He hadn't bothered to think, but he knew the answer. "Research. What else?"

There would be a lot of research done here. It had been suppressed too long, and had piled up a back-pressure that would have to be relieved. And from that research, he suspected, would come the end of the stable oligarchy of Earth. It could never stand against the changes that would be pouring out of Mars.

She put her hands on his shoulders and moved forward to kiss him. He bent down to meet her, and found her eyes were wet. Maybe his were, too. Then she broke free.

"You're a fool, Dan Feldman," she whispered, and

began moving down the hallway and out of the council hall of Mars.

Doc Feldman nodded slowly as he let her go. He was a fool. He had always been a fool, and always would be. And that was why he could never take over leadership here. Fools and idealists should never govern a world. It took practical men such as Jake to do that.

But the practical men needed the foolish idealists, too. And maybe for a time here on Mars their kind of men and his kind of fools could make one more stab at the ancient puzzle of freedom.

Outside the war rockets of Earth began landing quietly on the free soil of Mars.